"Emergency," came Julian's low staccato. "Malika is out."

You would expect the static of the dozen radios we had stashed all over our 55-acre campus, but only silence followed.

Christine stood up to look out my window and grabbed for her radio.

"Julian, this is Christine….How out is she?"

There was always the possibility she'd only gotten to an outer enclosure, behind just one locked chain-link gate rather than the much safer two or three.

Then we'd have a few tense minutes waiting for her to be escorted back in, but not much else —
like we had when Yi-ku had gotten out over the summer.

Another second followed and I looked around for the gun and the tasers.
We really should have had those things taped to the wall.

Then the static of Julian's radio for a few seconds,
then some more silence.

Then, over the radio: "Out out," Julian said. "Gone."

© Kim MacQueen
Published July 2011 by Jungo Books
ISBN 978-0-615-48182-1
kimmacqueen.com
jungobooks.com

Cover design by Chuck Badland
Cover photo by Kim Round
Author photo by Beverly Frick

Out,
Out

a novel of women and apes by **Kim MacQueen**

She says they talk back.

It's strange how often stories start in cars, how a little Honda could take you in minutes from the grey steel and graffiti of downtown, where your family sleeps up at the top of a big brick building, and drop you in the land of the lost. Funny if you start with the glare and steel of the interstate and then the roads start getting smaller and darker, their pools of black oil spreading further toward the grass with every mile south, how you can lean just a little to the right, roll off the main road and deep into woods so green you can't see the sun.

I drove up to the ape lab gate the first morning and stepped out, holding the car door across my body almost like a shield, to see that even the air was different here. It was heavy, still. A slick brown carpet of wet leaves lay there like a bed for my car, sucking up all the sound. Thick moisture covered everything outside the ten-foot metal gate, wrapping itself around me as I stood there wondering how to get in. Wet sticks from high up in the canopy were suspended in midair, caught in lower branches before they could reach the ground, dangling like steak knives.

The gate looked like it hadn't opened for anyone in years. Greying pine needles stuck out of the rusty tines, and sticks and leaves gummed up the underneath, impaled on the fencing's jagged edges. Up on the left at the gate's edge was a little metal box, about the size of a sandwich, looking like an old drive-in speaker with punch-in number keys like a phone, but I didn't have a code. I just stood there staring at it, wondering what to do, when the whole big thing clanged to life and swung toward me, its metal scraping the rutted road, gathering dead leaves like a windshield wiper. They knew I was coming. I had to jump in and move the Civic back ten feet or let it just take off the bumper. Then there was nothing to do but get in and drive through the gate, very slowly, toward my impromptu job interview.

Overgrown pine forest blocked out the light, and everything was amazingly lush, warm, soft and spongy. Fig trees sported leaves you could wear as a hat, so low to the ground they looked like seats for kids. Furry magnolia leaves held up creamy white flowers as big as dinner plates, and lichen climbed up the trees and spread out toward the road, slowly colonizing the place. The sound of cicadas drowned out my NPR.

It was like the forest closed around me, a thick green envelope pulling me in as it encircled my car. A hawk swooped down from a huge pine overhead. I heard the soft whoosh of her feathers just above the hood. Then she flew off to the side and scooped up some little screeching bird. A few seconds later, a deer glanced at me before it vanished into thick woods. I'd been on the grounds less than five minutes.

About a mile up the road, nearly hidden in the brush, was a nondescript one-story, concrete-block building, with a light cover of mold forming at the ground and creeping up its grey painted walls. Wet sticks and branches lay dead on beds of pine straw on the roof.

Behind the building rose a 30-foot tower made of chain link and plumbing pipes. An adult male chimpanzee with arms like hairy battering rams swung up to the top of the tower as I pulled up in the car. He was huge even from where I sat frozen in front of the steering wheel, 50 feet away.

I jumped in my seat as he started to yell. For a single second he sounded a little like the creaky gate, then he rounded out into oohs and explosive ahhs, quick bursts that were like being pelted with big balls of sound: "ooh ooh ooh oohwah oowah oohWAH oohWAH OOHWAH!"

It took me a few seconds, sitting staring up at him with my hands clutching my chest and my mouth hanging open, to realize that he wasn't trying to scare me away. He was announcing my arrival. He was an interspecies butler.

I pulled into the parking lot in front of the low Main building, thinking about the *Washington Post* article that had brought me here.

CONVERSATION: Soraya Baldwin-Ruhl
She Talks to Apes, and She Says They Talk Back

ATLANTA: Soraya Baldwin-Ruhl, 35, a researcher at Southern University outside of Atlanta, studies communication among primates and runs a 55-acre laboratory where she trains animals and humans to communicate with each other. She is the author of *Friends with Faraji: Communication with Sentient Apes*, published by Southern Universities Press.

Q. When the apes point to symbols on the computer, how can you tell that they're actually communicating?

A. We use words that they have learned the meanings of, that have corresponding symbols on the computer keyboard. Then we test them by either saying the words in English or by showing them pictures of the things we're talking about. There are a few apes at the lab who have not been taught to use language — control subjects — and those apes can't do the exercises at all.

Q. What do you say to your critics, who charge that the apes are simply mimicking you?

A. But they don't just repeat what we say. They come up with novel requests and they answer our questions. Of course, there's a little mimicry — like you might have when talking to a child. But according to our data, that's only about two percent of what they say.

Q. What about people who charge that you overstate the apes' abilities?

A. I have heard that a few people have said that, and I have invited our detractors to visit the lab and see firsthand what Faraji and the other apes here can do. None of them have done that. They seem to think that they already know that the apes can't do what we say they can, and so they don't need to come here and not see it for themselves. It's just crazy.

I can tell you that if these people did come and spend time with the apes who live here, if they did get to know them and see for themselves what these apes can do, then these people would understand. They would no longer be detractors.

I was working as a public relations specialist at the university's downtown campus when I got word that Dr. Baldwin-Ruhl needed someone at the ape lab to help with administration and public relations. The lab was ten miles off campus, south of town in the woods. When I asked people downtown what they actually did with the apes out there, nobody could tell me. After a couple days of asking around, somebody dug up the *Post* article for me.

A few who had met Soraya talked vaguely about the apes' language abilities but acknowledged that they didn't actually vocally form English words themselves. So they could tell me that the apes communicated, but not how.

Some secretary at human resources downtown gave me bad directions that cost me 20 minutes and I had to call from a decrepit gas station to clarify where the place was. The woman I'd come to know as Christine answered, her voice wispy over a staticky connection on an ancient pay phone.

"Where are you?" I yelled into a gummy, disgusting receiver.

"What?" Chrisine yelled back.

"Where are you?" I yelled again.

"What?" She yelled again, laughing now.

I still made it out there by lunchtime. It happened that they'd called on a Monday, the day after the Sunday *London Times* had visited the lab. The newspaper had run a full color, above-the-fold on 1A photo of a young ape cuddling a red rubber ball. His eyes were warm, brown saucers and they stared interspecies cuteness and love out at readers all over the world. The story described the writer meeting Joie, the two year-old bonobo ape in the picture, and carrying him around on his shoulder during the visit.

Christine had called me at my desk downtown later that morning. She said she'd stopped counting at 66 news outlets that had contacted the lab — an Australian 60 Minutes-style news show, *OK!* magazine in London and three radio stations in Africa — wanting follow-up interviews.

"We're out of our depth here," she said. "We've been talking for awhile about needing someone out here to deal with PR and paperwork, and then this. Can you come out today?"

Christine sounded so much like a little kid on the phone that I expected a really short person to meet me at the Main building that day. But when I finally found the wooded parking lot, tucked my Honda under a big, dripping oak and walked up to the lab's glass front door, the woman who met me was tall, friendly, blonde like me, her long hair tied back with a scrunchie. She wore a blue lab t-shirt and jeans, both with white holes from bleach splashes. She had a bandage around the last three fingers of her right hand. I didn't ask her anything about the bandage, and she didn't address it.

We sat down in the front office of the Main building by the receptionist's desk. She gave me the same introduction to the lab she gave to all visitors, pulling out a full-color brochure, green and shiny like the leaves outside, with head-and-shoulder photos of the lab's resident ape family looking up at me: Faraji, Imena, Joie, Malika, apes all in order with their names under their photos like the ones you see of actors as you're paying to get into a play.

I recognized the next thing she handed me – the *Washington Post* interview where Soraya talked about "detractors" – and I nodded.

"I've seen that one," I said. "They sent it to us downtown."

Christine shrugged, smiling broadly.

"I figured you might as well know all about what you're getting into," she said, looking away, suddenly seeming jaded.

I didn't know how to ask about what that meant. It was the kind of unspoken assertion I figured I'd pick up on once I'd been there awhile. So far no one had offered me anything, and I hadn't even met Soraya yet. But I'd decided I was coming to work out here in the forest with this tall woman with the bleached-out jeans. I didn't really fit in downtown. I wasn't working on anything pressing. So why not?

"So I'll take you around to meet everybody in a little bit. Aren't you lucky!" Christine said. She let a little more of herself out to show me every minute we sat there, smiling. She rolled her eyes ever so slightly as her radio barked at us from her hip pocket, a student announcing he'd be taking an ape from one building to the other. She switched it off for the rest of our talk.

"So what about this job?" I finally asked her.

She shrugged.

"I'm not sure. Soraya says we need someone to handle the money and sort of run interference between the lab and the university, and between the lab and the press — especially the press."

She fully rolled her eyes here, the motion almost swirling her whole head, wiping her smile off her face.

"Since that story in the *London Times*, the phone has been ringing off the hook around here, with all these people, from everywhere — Africa, Australia, England, New York, you name it — wanting to come here and film her working with the apes," she jerked her head in the direction of the phone as we talked, and she was right; all its lights were lit up.

"For awhile Soraya tried to set up all the press visits herself. There were like a hundred of them. It was a nightmare. Of course Soraya just lets them all come. She won't be a gatekeeper. Then they all get here at the same time and we're mobbed, and nobody's in control of the situation. Like I said: a nightmare."

She seemed to realize she might be scaring me then.

"But it'll be great. You can handle that stuff no problem. You're from downtown — that's a big scary world to some people here. The apes are pretty impressed by people from the city, too. They'll like you. It'll be fine. It'll be great. You'll see."

"But that's all I can really tell you about the job. You'll have to ask her what she wants," she said. Was I imagining her leaning on 'her,' rueful, almost bratty, like a child upset with her mother?

"Are you ready to go back and see her?" she asked me.

Now it's all over. Now Soraya isn't in my life. Now when I

remember, when I go back sometimes to the moment Christine asked me this, I usually think about how I could have just stood up then and just left. Made up some excuse and gotten back into my car and gone back to my apartment, untouched, uncorrupted. How righteous it would have been to just go home to my family and not get sucked into the bowels of that building toward her.

When I first met Marc, it was like that. He was a graduate student in forestry research then. It thrilled me to walk in the woods with him and hear the names of everything around us, to see grasses and trees as living beings that he knew about and could tell me. Facts that bounced off my forehead, that wouldn't go in, that I never needed to really grasp because he knew them. We were towheaded twins with big floppy cotton hats and shirts with long sleeves to protect our light skin from the sun. It was exciting, holding both his hands and looking into his face and knowing there was more in his head than I could ever see on the surface.

Now we had a little blonde girl together. Now I knew what he knew. He wasn't in research anymore and we fought over whose turn it was to make dinner, and I never held both his hands anymore, never got close enough to look into his face because I already knew what I'd see there.

But there wasn't any feeling to warn me about what was going to happen next. I didn't know what I was walking into. I didn't know. Seeing her for the first time was like the bottom dropping out of a wet paper bag. At that moment, everything was all over.

I remember that at the time, in those few minutes before I saw her, it felt like queing up to see a closeted former movie star, someone vain and unpredictable, not quite to be trusted. Christine made Soraya sound like a juvenile delinquent. So many times I've wondered how I might have reacted to Soraya if Christine hadn't acted like a spoiled younger sister around her. And then I remember: Soraya knocked me down. Punched me out like a prizefighter. Little sister wouldn't have stood a chance.

Christine walked me to the door of Soraya's office and hung back, a hand on the small of my back to push me forward.

Before Soraya I was as straight as I could be. When I met Marc in school, there was no whirlwind courtship, just a slow, methodical dance toward marriage. We'd had Chloe almost two years ago, and that's when I figured out what being married was for. After Soraya I am straight again. Straight. It sounds so dry and cool and measured. So normal. In between before and after is the bad time, the hurricane, the flood.

In the pictures, even the black and white candid shots taken outside with Faraji that ran with the newspaper articles, even in lab t-shirts and sweatpants and no makeup, she is beautiful. She has long, wavy, chocolate hair, dark eyes, olive skin. She looks Italian or maybe Middle Eastern. She's small, with a childlike body in jeans, always in boots and t-shirts, looking like she's just come in from the woods, ready at any moment to head back out.

She rose from her desk when I walked in, the light in her eyes intelligent and violent at the same time. She stuck out her hand to shake mine, and I saw the top digit of the index finger of her right hand was gone. But like Christine, she didn't address it, so neither did I. I didn't want to stare at her hand, so I looked quickly up at her face, and that was like getting rocks thrown at me. So I fixed my eyes at a spot on the wall behind her, a photo of her at the base of a mountain, arms akimbo, smiling broadly, friends all around her.

Her dark corner office smelled like a dog, lined with bookshelves and African art. Blankets heaped on the floor were covered with thick black animal hair. Some of the strands stood up by themselves, waving a little in the air conditioning. A six-foot Lexan window overlooked an ape's empty bedroom. A gorilla mask, bigger than a human man's head, sat on a shelf next to a grey and white mass of fake fur and beige lining and a freaky-looking bunny head.

She is the sort of person who answers the questions asked, and only those questions. I remember thinking that if I could just formulate the right question for her, she would — quietly, thoughtfully, and only if I didn't ever make any sudden movements — open the doorway and usher me into another world. She told a journalist in one magazine article that I'd read that she wasn't sure she was more human or more ape. Now I think I might have loved her before I ever saw her. But I don't know.

Her power comes mostly when you're in the same room with her. Then when you want her and you can't find her, when you're looking for a detail about her to tell yourself and you can't remember, you just make it up, and pretty soon you have a whole other Soraya that you concocted in your mind, made from whole cloth, who never existed.

Now when I look back on that time, I think about this little pool they had at the gym, only about 12 feet around but with scary-strong jets under the water, supposed to help you build up your muscles as you swam against a current so strong it would whip you around and smash you against the walls of the pool if you weren't careful. Marc called it the Swirling Vortex of Death. Now that I don't ever see Soraya any more, I wonder sometimes how I got sucked in so fast.

There she was, looking down at a messy desk, bushy bangs covering a childlike face. They had plenty of help taking care of the apes, she told me. That wasn't the problem. They needed help taking care of the people who took care of the apes.

Soraya had written three books and two monographs in the last several years; she had a lot of papers at various points in the academic pipeline. But she said she had little time these days for paper of any kind.

"I don't know how I'm going to return all these calls, let alone what I'd tell the people when I spoke to them. They all want to come here, to re-interview all of us and get their own footage, spend weeks here. More than 60 news organizations. They can't all just come. It's so disruptive to the research and to the apes' lives. We don't have enough staff to deal with all this. You've got to help us!" she laughed, and I felt like she'd grabbed my heart and my stomach in one hand, thrown them up into the air, started juggling them. Oh, I am in trouble, I thought, I'm dead, and the thought doesn't scare me nearly as much as it should.

On her desk was a yellow legal pad with a long list of names and numbers on it, the curling pages covered in girly longhand. She handed it to me and looked up at me, into my face. It was shocking, a recognition, very like the moment I first saw my daughter.

I was 35 at the time. I'd had so many stupid office jobs, so many positions so different yet so much the same, where I felt superfluous, like my colleagues belonged there but they were all graciously making space for me. But Soraya needed someone. She'd reached out of the sky and picked me. I watched her realize I was the one she needed. The thought spread out across her face, softening it, lightening it. I was already helping. She was already starting to think she needed me.

She asked me about myself. I told her about Marc, about Chloe, who was 18 months old then, our move from Maryland when Marc lost his job. She paid attention to every word, her face softening at all the right places. The interview felt more like a date.

One of the apes was pregnant, about to go off any minute, but they didn't really know when it would happen, when she'd gotten pregnant or exactly how long bonobo gestation periods were. So Soraya had brought a cot into her office and moved in. She had a cell phone and email but said she hadn't looked at either one in a week. She sat back down at her desk, where tall, neat paper piles surrounded her on both sides.

It occurred to me then that when she said she'd moved in at the lab, she meant the ape enclosure. Her dark hair was tied up in a messy ponytail and her skin had a warm patina that made her glowy. There were little bits of dried grass on her teal blue t-shirt. If she looked like she was living with Leakey in the field in Africa, it was because she'd woken up that morning on the floor of a cage with an ape.

I took a seat in a leather chair across from her and watched her talk. It was so quiet there, so natural. A black lab wandered in and sat at Soraya's feet. She called him Bob and scratched his ears while she talked to me. Her office felt more like a home than the two-bedroom Buckhead apartment Marc and Chloe and I knocked around and warmed up bottles and microwavable dinners in, where we hadn't gotten around to hanging curtains or photos after seven months.

Once at a party, an artist friend of a friend had whipped up a pencil sketch of Marc and I sitting on the couch together. It was serene and simple. We're looking at our friend Maria as she reads a poem. We'd had it framed after the wedding and set on the mantel in our little apartment near the university. I thought about it as I looked around Soraya's office at candid photos, framed certificates and dark, intricate abstract drawings plainly made by apes. I thought of our drawing back at the apartment, that it must be in one of the boxes we hadn't unpacked yet.

Not many of them were. After Marc got laid off from his forestry research position at the university in College Park — grant ended, nobody's fault, they were so sorry — we hadn't packed up and left so much as floated slowly south, ending up in Atlanta, settling in a big beige apartment off the interstate like flotsam from the road. Now he sold cell phones, traipsing off to work in the mall every day in khakis and an off-white polo with the store's name on it. The drab of his clothes matched his own colors exactly, picking up the ruddy, raw-looking places in his face, making him look washed out, vacant-eyed, vaguely pissed off.

Then BAM! as the bloated belly and four foot long, bodybuilder arms of an ape hit the window and hung there, stretched spread-eagle, staring at me from across the room.

"That's Faraji," Soraya said. Then she faced the window. "Faraji, you're being rude."

"He can hear you say that through that thick glass window?"

Soraya nodded and spoke slowly, her eyes on me.

"They can hear everything we say, no matter where we are, on this whole complex. Even way out in the woods, out there ourselves with them back here, locked up in there, they can hear what we say," she whispered. Bonobos possess hearing far beyond what we humans have, she said, nodding in his direction.

"He knows you're a nice person because you and I are sitting here talking together," she said. "He can tell you're a friend. If I got angry, if I stood up and waved my arms and wanted to throw you out…he'd be upset. He'd want to bite you."

My neck felt stiff and strange. I wanted to turn around and stare at Faraji but I didn't want to be afraid of him. I just looked at Soraya. She spoke about Faraji like he was a human man, her friend or brother.

"He's motioning to you," Soraya said, and I finally turned and watched as Faraji crooked a flaky, black finger at me. "He wants you to come over there and say hello."

I walked over to the window, the ape's eyes like high-beam headlights on only me. Most of his body was huge and black, but at the moment he was displaying his stomach and greyish underarms, manlike and covered thinly with four-inch, course black hair. His swollen belly pressed up against the glass, and he had fingers that grew about a foot out of a black palm before curling to sharp nails, cracked and dirty ebony. A little more pressure on the window, I thought, and he'd bring the whole wall down.

I finally looked at his face. A little like a chimpanzee, but then not really. Where chimpanzee faces are light brownish, bonobos are black. With tiny eyes like bright brown beads in the water, that saw me and knew me in an instant.

"Faraji is Swahili for comfort," came Soraya's voice behind us.

I'd never really looked into the eyes of an ape before. I knew animal-crazy women who lovingly deposit spiders outside the front door to save their lives or let the dog sleep on the bed. I was not one of them. Marc and I had Pippi, a Pomeranian he'd gotten at the pound before we were married, but I didn't spend a whole lot of time with her. She'd get so lonely while we were at work that she'd eat the garbage, leaving it strewn all over the living room floor. I would yell at her, and she would just cower and stare at me with her pleading dog eyes. I'd sweep up the mess and not speak to her for days.

"Don't stare at him, Deb, you'll upset him," came Soraya's voice.

I didn't think so. With his eyes, his steady gaze, Faraji looked back to tell me he couldn't have cared less what I did.

We looked at each other through the two-inch, hard plastic, metal-reinforced wall. His eyes would scan my face and flick away, shiny and beady in hoody black lids. He looked like a plastic and paper mache animal diorama I'd come across in a museum, a living exhibit-being, bored by the dozens like me who came to check him out every day.

I realized as I looked at Faraji that he'd been the one trying to scare me, hanging spread-eagled on the wall. Daring me to look back at him. That made me stare more balefully at him, telling him, just through looking, that he couldn't. And I think he picked up on that, so he dismissed me, fell back off the wall and crouched down on the floor with his long ape arms falling between his knees, looking again at his nails.

Soraya seemed to be outside of us then. I didn't know whether she was watching or not. But I knew she was trying to gauge my fear too. I had a little bit of it down there somewhere, what felt to me like a healthy, respectful amount for being in the proximity of an animal who could crush me easily. But I learned in that moment never to let either of them see it, and it worked. It felt like those first seconds after I ran Marc's car into a tree in our neighbor's yard, or right after someone slaps you across the face. That thing that you were dreading has happened. You focus, realize you're still standing upright, take a breath and go from there.

What scared me the most back then was my own daughter. Chloe wasn't two yet, my first, and I loved her so completely and thoughtlessly that it seemed impossible she wouldn't die, horribly and very soon.

Nothing was wrong with her. She wasn't sick. She was healthy and happy and smart, in no danger. She was soft and warm and golden and she was my whole heart, who woke up singing her little baby songs every morning. But every time we took her picture, every time someone gave me a blanket or a toy for her, I'd think of the inevitable time I'd see those things after she was gone and how it would blow up my heart like a bomb.

I spent every drive to the grocery store imagining elaborate scenarios where she would be killed or maimed or taken from me forever. Within a few days of her being born, I decided that if anything really bad ever did happen to her I'd have to commit suicide pretty much within the hour.

I put off having a second child because I knew once I had two, if I lost one of them, I'd have to wait some respectable amount of time before I could kill myself. Her birth had given me, and only me, the ability to see and mourn for a desolate future without her.

I kept this up for two years. But I didn't plan on bringing Chloe to the ape lab, so the apes could only ever hurt me, not her. And I didn't care what happened to me.

2

He goes along with it for her.

Her hold on me started that first day, a sickish nervous energy like a boa-constrictor squeeze around my midsection, making me not want to eat. I looked at my arms barely shaking on the steering wheel as I drove from downtown every morning — already bony, barely there. White skin, blonde hairs the whole way down my arm. If the light shone through the windshield just right you could almost see through the whole thing, it was like a skinned chicken.

My first mornings on the job started hot and sticky, 90 degrees before 9 a.m. I hurried each day from the temperature-controlled air of my car to the lab's front door, huddled under the canopy of the leaves above, already tired before I ever got started. Then I opened the heavy glass door and stepped into a cloud of cool, dry air and the calming hum of the industrial-sized air conditioner.

On one of those first mornings, Christine had left a videotape on my chair, with "Watch Me" scrawled on a yellow sticky note. The tape was old, light like dry bones, with a faded, peeling label, its gluey backing all dried up. It looked like it might get caught in the workings of the VCR.

I found an old school-style TV cart in the conference room and pulled up a chair next to it. The tape held a homemade documentary of Soraya's work with Faraji. As it got going, I realized its setting was the same view I'd get if I stood up on a chair and looked past the TV, through the Lexan window looking into the ape area: a big, grey, square concrete-block room built to house a family of bonobos. The researchers still call it the living room.

The tape begins with a scene of the two of them sitting there together. She sits cross-legged in jeans and a red ribbed t-shirt, cut to fit her body but comfortable. The date stamp on the video is 6/5/1981. She's in her early twenties, thin, flexible. She sits cross-legged on the floor, sneakered feet tucked under her knees. Her name flashes in red underneath her on the screen: Soraya Baldwin-Ruhl, professor of biology.

Her hair is the color of chocolate bars, curling over her shoulders and creeping down her back. Faraji is knee-to-knee with her. The camera comes in for a close-up on his face, shiny black with brown eyes. I thought again how like a chimpanzee's his face was, but how different: smaller, the features sharper.

"Bonobos look more human than chimpanzees do," Christine had told me. "They're really closer genetically to us than they are to chimpanzees."

I stared at Faraji on the TV screen now. Text running under his face read: Faraji, Bonobo, *Pan paniscus*.

The camera pans to include them both. Her dark brown eyes focus only on him. They make conversation for a moment.

"Faraji, can you show me the ball?" she asks him.

Faraji stares at her, hesitating for just a second. Of course he can show her the ball. It's as though he's waiting for her to give him something more difficult to do. If he had eyebrows, you can almost picture him raising them at her like an insolent teenager, and it's only when he doesn't that he begins to seem not human. His all-black face is impassive as he scoops up the ball with a hairy arm, as wide at the bicep as a man's head. He sets it down in front of her.

"Good!" She sounds like she's talking with a four-year old human boy. "Now, can you show me the doggy?"

There's a six-inch-long stuffed dog behind Faraji, possibly a plaything for the younger apes. He can't see it. He looks around a minute, peers over his left shoulder, spots it, then palms it and holds it up to her.

"Good!" She's beaming at him. "Now, can you show me the snake?"

Same thing. This time the item she desires is across the room, black and yellow rubber lying against the grey concrete wall. He lazily crosses the room, only now really starting to move like an actual ape you might see at the zoo, swinging arms as long as his legs, covered with soft, black shiny hair, maneuvering on knuckles curled into easy fists. He picks up the snake, brings it to her.

"Great, Faraji, thank you! Now…can you make the doggie *bite* the snake?"

Faraji sits back down, gets comfortable. Takes the plastic snake and puts it in the dog's mouth. Sets them both down on the floor in front of him and looks at her.

The voiceover starts then, an older man's voice, placing the two at the Southern University Primate Language Lab. At the time they tape was made, Faraji was about six years old, a male bonobo able to demonstrate understanding of at least 300 symbols as well as novel commands — like "make the doggie bite the snake" — on her request. He'd do it for other researchers too, if he knew them well, "but it always seems to work better for Dr. Baldwin-Ruhl," the voice-over said.

The footage cuts to a talking head-style interview of Soraya standing in the woods outside the lab, her head and shoulders taking up the screen as she squints a little in the sun and talks to the camera in a voice that's crisp and soft, girlish.

"We never set out to teach Faraji to communicate with us in English. It happened organically, more or less by accident. We were trying to teach his mother, Malika, to use the symbols on the computer keyboard that was developed here at the lab. The idea was to teach the apes to use the language symbol keyboard to communicate with us, to ask for things like food or permission to go outside. Faraji was always there, usually playing in a back corner of the room. We didn't even think he was paying attention."

Her voice-over continues: "Then one day when Faraji was about three years old, we took Malika out of the room, because she had to go see the vet. Faraji just went over to the computer keyboard and started pressing the buttons to ask for foods he liked, just as though he'd been doing it always."

Christine had told me that week that, after five years of trying to teach Malika to use the lexigrams to ask for food or to go outside — all the skills Faraji had picked up as a toddler ape, on the fly — they'd given up, blaming her lack of attention. She didn't seem to want to learn, and she didn't seem to be able to.

"They tracked her eye movements with the video camera," Christine said, "and they realized that she was scanning the place every second, running her eyes up and down the walls and over the doors every minute of every day, like she never really trusted that she was safe, like she never trusted that her children were safe. She still does that. She can't ever relax. We try to make sure the little ones are with her constantly because otherwise she starts acting nuts, charging the chainlink and screaming."

The video showed a still shot of a young Faraji, more shiny hair tufted on his boyish ape face, on a jaunt in the woods. He's walking upright, bowlegged, on a leash. Soraya's looking off-camera, pointing out something in the woods. The photo is from back before the development of his bodybuilder arms, and he gazes back over his shoulder into the camera. The shape of his body is like a walking frog, with knees and elbows bent out to the sides, turned out like a dancer.

Older footage followed, grainy footage of a babyish Faraji at a computer keyboard. He wears huge headphones covering the sides of his head while a researcher calls to him from inside a grey box the size of a telephone booth in the corner of the room.

"Faraji, can you point to the symbol for 'orange?' Point to the symbol for 'orange,'" comes the researcher's voice.

You can see Faraji point his tiny right index finger at something on the computer, and the computerized voice says "orange," over the loudspeaker.

"Good, Faraji, now can you point to the symbol for 'outside?' Point to the symbol for 'outside.'"

"Outside," says the computer's voice.

"Great job, Faraji!" the researcher can be heard clapping his hands from inside the box. Faraji gives himself a hand too.

Then the narrator is silent as another outdoor scene unfolds. Faraji is sitting cross-legged on a path through the woods behind the main building. He's flint-knapping, fashioning tools from stone like the ancient Indians did. The sun shines on his black fur and his big bodybuilder arms klick-klick-klick the two rocks together to make a spearhead.

Its audience now updated on his early history, the video returns to Soraya and an older Faraji at the time of the taping, still sitting cross-legged together on the floor.

"Faraji, can you make the doggy bite the snake?"

Sure he can. Only a little clumsily, the ape takes the stuffed dog in one hand and the rubber snake in the other, and puts the snake in the dog's mouth.

"That's great, Faraji."

Soraya stops now, rests her hands on her knees. Faraji looks at her, and you almost expect him to look as a dog might, playful, ready for the next round. Instead he leans back on his haunches and eyes her almost warily. Like they're a longtime couple on a date, away from the kids for the first time in awhile. He's going along with it for her, because life will be better for him if he does.

She does something unsettling now — reaches behind her and puts on a huge, gun-metal grey-brown welder's mask. It takes her a moment to secure it and set it straight on her face. But Faraji looks used to this too. He studies the nails on his right hand while he waits.

A voice-over guy explains that a few of Baldwin-Ruhl's critics have charged that Faraji's just watching Soraya's face for clues, rather than really knowing the words. So she puts on a welder's mask, which completely obscures her expression and thus takes away the possibility of subconscious cuing.

"Faraji," comes her muffled voice from behind the acromegalic mask. "Can you put the ball in the refrigerator?"

He loses no time crossing the room again, going to the mini-fridge at the edge of the room's L-shaped, against-the-wall kitchen, putting the red ball in and closing the door. She stops talking then, levels the mask to look right at the camera, and says nothing.

Sure he can do it, welder's mask or no. Now he does come right back, sit down and watch for her next move. It's like he wants to help her make this point.

22

I turned the tape off after this scene, vowing to watch it later. It suddenly seemed much more interesting to just watch Faraji — today's older Faraji, 26 — wander around in the next room.

I didn't know a thing about Faraji until I came to work for the lab, but he's famous among schoolchildren who are interested in apes and in countries like Japan. I never really got to the bottom of it during the entire time I worked there, but the Japanese are fascinated with apes. They love Faraji, who they watched grow up on documentaries made by NHK Television, one every few years released there during the time he was growing up. They recognize him, much more so than Americans do, as the first ape in the world to understand spoken English.

I couldn't get a good view of the ape room just by looking through the window, so I dragged my chair over to the window and stood on it. Then I could see him, lying just under the window on the other side. He didn't seem to see me. He was lying on his back, looking at his nails just like he'd done on the tape.

Quickly and quietly, he got up and walked on all fours across the room, through a three-foot metal door, and climbed up a chain-link wall to a loft high in the ceiling. He moved like dancing, rocking and fluid, comfortable in his skin, just the slightest bit bored. How funny that the narrator on the tape kept comparing Faraji's abilities to those of a two-and-a-half year old human child when he was bigger than most men. His round, muscular shoulders were as wide as two high school football players standing side by side.

The overhead lights caught his thick black hair and made it shine. He had a male pattern baldness thing going on now that wasn't there when the tape was made. Once up in the loft, he sat heavily on his haunches and very slowly, unblinkingly, swung his head around and stared at me.

It made me suck in my breath. He had seen me after all. He'd just headed up to the loft so he'd have a better vantage point to look back.

3

My stomach flipped when I said her name.

Soraya never came to my house. But I felt her there almost immediately, as I sat with Marc and Chloe eating dinner. The ghost of her was sitting there with us, between Chloe and me. When I looked across our little dining room table at Marc I saw Soraya instead, the outline of her dark hair like a window I had to look through to see him, so much that I shook my head, squeezed my eyes shut and tried again. I had to make myself see Marc actually sitting there, thin and blonde in a washed-out yellow t-shirt, spooning mashed potatoes onto Chloe's plate. Normal. Content in a way I suddenly couldn't manage anymore.

Marc asked Chloe about school, trying to move the conversation along because I was suddenly afraid to speak at all. He'd tied up her hair into blonde ringlets, ponytails on each side of her head like Cindy Brady. She didn't seem to feel like talking either. I just stared at her, looking through her buttery skin, her corduroy jumper, her crepe-soled kids' Mary Janes bumping rhythmically against the table legs. Why when I looked at my beautiful girl did I suddenly see the face of a woman? It had never happened before. Marc had always been enough before. Now suddenly he wasn't. The realization hit me while I watched Chloe eat mashed potatoes, while I stared at her pink plastic milk cup, wanting to throw up.

I was afraid Marc would ask me about my new job, and then he did. So I looked right at Chloe and started talking about the apes. She looked quizzically at me, thinking of the plastic ape toys she had in her bedroom, that had come in a tube with monkeys and palm trees that she made play with her Barbies. The Barbies were three times bigger than the plastic apes, so the Barbies pushed the apes around a lot. She didn't seem to understand why I would go to work and apes would be there.

"I think it's like a zoo," Marc said to her, with a desperate look at me to help him explain. But I couldn't. I said it wasn't really like a zoo, and no Chloe couldn't come visit there and meet the apes – and here I threw Marc a withering look for making her think maybe she could one day. I never told either one why they never could. They never could because they'd need tuberculosis tests just to get in the front door, as apes are super-susceptible to TB. They never could because these weren't zoo apes we were dealing with. They were dangerous.

But I couldn't look at Marc. At the time I didn't know whether or not he realized it. Of course now I know he did.

It was an office job. I had my own big, airy space, with an Egyptian rug I'd brought from home and a huge window overlooking the parking lot, which was lined with old-growth trees that stretched down to the river and blocked out the light. As business manager, I did the paperwork to hire new lab assistants, buy supplies, and keep Soraya's paycheck deposits going steadily into her checking account, even as she slipped from regular semester teaching load to summer pay and had to hopscotch across three different federal grants to pay everything from her salary to the electric bill. I kept the credit card bills straight, chasing down receipts for blankets and food and toys that staff members tended to leave crumpled on the floors of the vehicles, trampled by several pairs of dirty hiking boots.

During that first week I started inventing reasons to go back to Soraya's office. She wasn't there often. I would creep into the quiet dark of her space, and then look over my right shoulder, through the window of the apes' bedroom. Sometimes she was over in the kitchen area making food for Faraji and Imena and Malika while they laid around and played with the baby apes. Sometimes she'd just be there talking to them, sitting on the floor with Faraji while Joie careened around the place. The window was waist-high, and if she was sitting on the floor of the ape enclosure I knew she couldn't see me sitting in her office. So one afternoon I just sat at her desk in the dark, just sat there, looking around at her books and blankets and papers in the half-light, knowing she was just in the next room. I sat in her world and she didn't even know it, I thought, she doesn't even know it.

I was also the lab's gatekeeper. If someone wanted to visit the apes, to write about them for some TV show or media outlet or just because they'd heard about Soraya's work with them and wanted to meet either her or them, they had to go through me.

Julian Arroyo, Soraya's postdoc, had the office next to mine. He'd been with her several years. He was thin and quiet, wiry. He was probably in his late 20s, with the unsettled air of a longtime student. He had an easy, happy way with the apes. He gave me the feeling he took a lot on himself, like maybe he assured Soraya that things were fine and hung out in ape cages or hunched over his laptop until midnight making it that way. He wasn't married and made jokes about living out of his truck anyway.

It was Julian who gave me the gatekeeper role the day we met. He leaned against the doorjamb in my office, lanky and relaxed, like standing up straight took too much trouble. His long black hair was tied into a ponytail. He traced his sneakered toe along the floor as we talked.

"This is so awesome," he said. "We need a buffer between the apes and the animal rights nutjobs, and you're it," he said it light and jokey-like, but he was serious. We had a relaxed connection from that first day. He made me laugh every time I talked to him.

"I'm a buffer?" I giggled. "I don't think I know how to be a buffer."

"It's easy. I'm sure you've noticed we don't have any business cards or letterhead with our address or direct phone number on it, and physical location wasn't listed on the lab's website. If they knew where we were, they'd swing by en masse to try to spring the apes from their cages. It's happened before," he said warily.

Christine had mentioned the day before that we had to use the campus address downtown for everything, so all the mail was days to weeks late getting to us. I just hadn't thought to ask why. Vendors were often very pissed off at us before we even received their bills, she said. It was a problem.

Most days we all had lunch together in the big conference room while Julian and his student assistants copied tapes from the previous day's research session and made notes. Christine prepared a special lunch for the apes every day to make sure Faraji stayed on his low-carb diet. After she was finished, she'd sit down with us and eat her own sandwich from home.

During those lunches, I eventually met everyone at the lab I didn't normally come into contact with every day. My office was in the entrance area, and they spent most of their time in the ape areas in the back of the building, so we didn't all see each other much during the workday, unless I was slinking around the halls trying to find Soraya, or they came up front to sign forms or turn in receipts.

There were cousins from Congo: Uba Youlou and Kalala Moaena, who I'd met hurriedly in the hall only once before. Uba lived in a trailer on the lab grounds. He was big as Kalala was little, both of them coal-black, grown children of Congolese diplomats who had emigrated to the U.S. to work in ape conservation. Uba and Kalala worked as ape caretakers and Ardelle was the lab's receptionist, and the three of them were the only blacks in Soraya's lab. They were so beautiful, so dark and exotic. I felt bland next to them, waiflike and inconsequential.

If you worked at the lab and you were from Africa, you were generally given an American-sounding nickname, so Kalala was actually called Clara.

"It was Soraya's idea. She just thinks it's easier," Christine said, sunny, shrugging.

"I like the name Clara," Kalala/Clara said sweetly, taking a peanut butter sandwich out of a plastic bag.

But Uba was just Uba.

"I guess she figured Uba was easy enough," Christine said. She'd grown up in South Georgia, learning about land and animals from peanut-farming parents. She'd been with Soraya six years.

"I came to Atlanta to work with apes, not famous women scientists," she joked that first week. She was offhand and ironic, joking in public and probably sweating the details privately, hardest on herself. Everything out of her mouth had a double meaning.

One Wednesday during the mindless chatter you have during

daily lunch with co-workers, I wondered aloud if I was cut out for the job. I was already bored silly from a morning of paperwork, and I was complaining and rubbing my eyes. Even while I spoke, though, I knew I was more cut out for paperwork than I would have been working in the back with the apes like my new colleagues or spending my days at home with Chloe.

When we'd first gotten to Atlanta, Marc's idea had been that he'd try to scare up work at the U.S.D.A. Forestry Service research station near the Chattahoochee River. He didn't get any answers to an intro email his former supervisor sent on his behalf, so one day during the first few weeks we were in Atlanta, he put on a suit and went down there.

I sat on the couch giving Chloe a bottle while he got ready, facing the TV, watching her start falling asleep in anticipation of her morning nap, my back to Marc as he struggled to straighten his tie.

"You know, if I was to go to work with the Forestry Service, maybe you wouldn't have to work at all. You could stay home with Chloe," he said, nearly out of breath, pacing and straightening.

I jerked my head up, feeling the horror of that idea cross my face. There was no way I wanted to stay home with Chloe. I just knew something terrible would happen if I did. Going mad with boredom would be the best outcome. I turned slightly so he couldn't see my face, pretended I hadn't heard him, pretended to watch TV.

He came back just a couple of hours later. He would never tell me what had or hadn't happened. The next day he drove up to Perimeter Mall and got a job selling cell phones.

So far, I loved my job. I couldn't wait to get there in the morning to hear the chimpanzees hoot-greet me from their plumbing-pipe perches. The chimps belonged to another lab on our campus, to a part-time faculty member who did memory research. We didn't spend any time with the other lab's staff or animals, but just having them there made me feel like I was part of a huge effort that encompassed the whole animal world.

"I just sit at my desk and fill out forms, and I know at the back of the building you guys are making videos and running research trials and writing papers, and it seems a lot more interesting than what I'm doing," I carped at lunch that day.

Julian took out a sheet of paper and started drawing a diagram for me.

"Here are the apes," he said, drawing a long box on the bottom of the sheet. On the row above, he drew several smaller boxes. "Here are the caretakers, like Clara over there," he nodded to her as she cut up cherry tomatoes, and she beamed. He wrote Clara's name in a box.

"Here's me and Christine and Uba," drawing three more boxes another level up. He put their names in the boxes.

He drew one small box on the next level up.

"That's Soraya," I said, feeling self-conscious and stupid almost immediately. My stomach did a flip when I said her name.

"Yes, that's Soraya," he said. Then he drew another box above her. He put my name in it.

"What for?"

"You buy the food, Deb. You pay the bills. The apes know you're number one. Or they will once you've been here awhile."

Now I felt embarrassed.

"Truly," he said, turning back to his sandwich.

"How do they know, though? Do you tell them?"

"Sure. We tell them about what's going on at the lab every day. We say, 'Deb's doing the visitor logs today, or Deb's reconciling the credit cards today, so watch out! Get her your receipts! Things like that. You know."

I'd put my sandwich down after I said her name, suddenly not able to eat anymore. Soraya. It was a sound like a wave of dust and the cry of some tropical bird. I looked around, grateful that no one seemed to notice. That first week, saying her name made butterflies fly around in my stomach.

I enjoyed it the first few days, refusing to stop to think about what it meant. Now I started to feel sick. My body was unwilling to undergo any more stress at the sound of this woman's name without my mind taking a few minutes to figure out what the hell was going on.

I wasn't ready to do it at that lunch, though. I packed up my uneaten food and stuffed it back into my brown paper bag, taking all my stirrings and questions and nerves and shoving them in there and, for the moment at least, throwing them away.

And it was the next day that everything really got going.

I was at my desk when Christine called, telling me I needed to go out with her and "really learn the place." That turned out to mean touring the woods in the Jeep with her.

"We do a lot of work out here with them," she explained, driving the big vehicle over the rutted road, leafy branches scraping its sides. The faster she drove, the more they whipped into the windows and grazed my face. "We work in spots all over these woods. We're coming up on what Soraya calls the lean-to up here in a minute."

All I could see was woods, but then she turned a corner and there it was, a wooden lean-to with pine needles hanging down from its green corrugated plastic roof. And there suddenly was Soraya, sitting cross-legged on the ground. My heart stopped.

We parked the Jeep and went over to her. She was making notes in a green notebook the size of a paperback, and she smiled as we walked up. Christine's been here for years, I thought, Soraya wouldn't smile like that if just Christine walked up. Right? Right?

It was muggy out but still felt like spring yet, the light green leaves throwing sunlight in patches all around her. We walked up to her on the rocky road, covered with pine needles still crunchy from when it was cold.

Christine directed my attention back out around us now, pointing.

"So this is where we come with Faraji and Bunny sometimes. When Bunny comes, Faraji likes to come out and see him and they play —"

"Wait — Bunny?" I looked from Christine to Soraya and back. "Who's Bunny?"

"Bunny is Christine in a bunny suit," Soraya smiled.

Christine nodded. "The apes love it. It gives them something to do during the day, to come outside and talk to an exciting visitor. It's like kids sometimes do at their birthday parties. Soraya thought it up a couple of years ago and the apes just live for it. They love Bunny. He comes around every couple of weeks or so."

"And then there's Gorilla," Soraya added.

"That's why there's a gorilla mask in your office!" I squealed like a kindergartner, and was immediately embarrassed. I looked away from them.

"Gorilla doesn't come out very often," Christine said, slow and plaintive, like she was talking about a preschool game. "Gorilla's scary."

I forced myself to get back into the conversation, though I wanted to just run and hide.

"Wait, they're apes," I said, feeling stupid. "Why are they scared of another ape? When Christine puts on the gorilla costume, she's still not going to be as big as Faraji. Right? Why would he be scared?"

I looked pointedly to Soraya for an explanation.

"Well, sometimes the apes forget they're big and scary. They don't think of themselves that way. I think they see themselves more like little kids — and for the most part we talk to them as though that's what they are. They see Gorilla and they react like a child would. He's big and he tries to frighten them, and they're scared. That's why these costumes help us communicate with them. By dressing up as something else, we can let them know it's okay to be themselves," she said.

"So they don't realize that's just Christine in a gorilla suit?" I said, resigning myself to feeling stupid.

"No, they don't," Soraya said, smiling, shaking her head. "How would they?"

I was starting to realize just how different this was from going to see an ape in a zoo.

"And over there," Christine said, pointing to a clearing a little way down the rutted road, "that's where we go sometimes for picnics."

Soraya put out a hand to steady herself as she stood up.

"That reminds me," she said, rising gracefully, slowly. "I'm hungry. Isn't it about lunchtime?"

Christine unhooked her radio from her belt loop and used it to call Faraji, back at the main building.

"You want us to come back and bring you something good to eat?" she called to him.

The pant-hoots started slow and low, fifty feet away, then got louder and more crazy, escalating into a pitch that made my head pound and my blood race around in my veins.

We walked back to the building, Soraya stopping to pick some of the wild onions that Faraji himself had planted back in the fall.

The rising chorus of hooting was so loud we couldn't hear each other talk.

So I learned to expand my territory. When nobody was around, when paperwork got boring, when I needed to see just a glimpse of her so that I didn't feel like I was going to hyperventilate —I would get up and go slink around the hall to her office, and if she wasn't there, I'd go out the back door and walk through the woods. It was comforting to know I could be dealing with a vendor or an administrator downtown on the phone one minute, and lose myself in the woods the next minute.

I'd walk along by myself, hoping not to run into anybody else but maybe her if she happened to be out there, telling myself I wasn't actually looking for her; I was just out getting some air. I'd talk to her as if she were beside me. When she was actually with me I felt so ridiculous, so ham-handed. She led the conversation. By myself, in the woods, my mind flowed easily and I told her things, things I never got a chance to ever tell her in person. And every few minutes I'd talk to myself too, saying what am I doing, what the hell am I doing?

4

She thinks we don't know.

I was on the job a few weeks when Soraya asked me to get a letter out to a Dr. Terry Oakley, who ran a facility across town that used primates as subjects for biomedical research. I Googled him to get his address and found an animal rights website called "Terry Oakley is a Monster."

Below the headline was a grainy black and white photo of a tiny macaque monkey baby strapped inside a white box with a metal bar sticking out of the back of its neck. The fear and pain were right there in its eyes, its babyish eyes, eyes that looked like my little girl's. A face that looked a lot like hers at six months, fresh and new and open.

I had to get up from my desk and go outside and sit on the sidewalk, my back to the azalea hedge hugging my knees, trying not to be seen by the people walking inside from the parking lot, until I felt like I might not be sick. Ardelle looked up his address for me.

My mother, Phyllis, called on my cell phone at just that moment from New York.

"Marc says you're working where, now?" she said. "Some monkey place?"

Phyllis had always been amused by my long list of post-college jobs. I drifted listlessly for years through offices, restaurants, stores, and a couple of broke nonprofits before I got a job editing the alumni magazine for Fordham University in Manhattan. I thought that job might keep me happy forever, until two years later when the publication schedules and meetings and plans just started to seem so samey to me. Argue with the vice president over stupid idea after stupid idea. Call some alumnus, get their story and their photograph, knock out 1,600 words, work with the designer to punch the thing up so it looked like something, drive out to some printer's that used to be a suburban cornfield for middle-of-the night press checks and then spend the next three weeks haggling over the print bill.

I am not the type of person to call a vice president's ideas stupid just because he's an annoying wasp from Westport, Connecticut with a Napoleonic complex, descended from a long line of development men. But — by way of example — this man brought me the one single photograph of black people to run during my entire tenure at the magazine, a snapshot of rich white alumni on safari in Africa flanked by black men dressed as savages. I wish I could say I handed the photo back with a firm but polite No, but instead I took it from him and looked down at the floor, probably even smiled and thanked him. I held onto the photo until the next day, when I walked it back over to his chirpy blonde assistant and left it with her. Then I started plotting my next move.

The week after Marc started selling cell phones, I got a public relations job at Southern, placing unreturned phone calls to newspaper science writers for seven months. Then Soraya called.

"Honey," my mom said. "I don't know. So you're bored, fine, but I think you're supposed to move up, not around. I just can't picture you with monkeys."

"Apes."

"Apes. Well, what is the difference, really?"

I had just learned the difference a few weeks before.

"Apes don't have tails, Mom. Apes —"

"Listen, here's what I'm saying: You're bored, you do something at nights. Help somebody. Volunteer. Start working with Chloe, make her the first two-year old in the world who knows how to read. But you leave a perfectly good job in downtown Atlanta for apes out in the woods? For what? Isn't it dangerous?"

I didn't answer her. She waited a beat, then:

"Marc is worried about you. I talked to him the other day. Did he tell you?"

I still didn't answer.

"Well, he told me. I asked him what your job was at the lab and he said he didn't know. You never told him. What are you planning to do when Chloe asks you what you do for your job? Are you going to ignore her too?"

Try as I might, I can't really remember the rest of that conversation.

...

Most of the work at our lab was funded by the National Institutes of Health, based on the idea that bonobos can generally demonstrate the same proficiency of language as a three-year-old human child. They were also very creative, making music, painting and drawing, though the NIH wasn't as interested in their grasp of art and culture. The study focused on bonobos, since they're arguably more human-like even than chimpanzees. They have smaller, darker faces. They even walk more upright than chimpanzees do, though they still do the knuckle-drag thing common to all apes. They're also demonstrably smarter.

38

When you see chimpanzees or bonobos at the zoo, they're usually in big man-made habitats out in the open air, fields in Atlanta or San Diego designed to look like Africa. But the apes at our lab lived mostly indoors. A few had been repatriated from Congo, one had been a circus ape in Japan and one or two were gifts from the zoo. The rest had been born at the lab, in concrete-block bedrooms and chain-link outdoor enclosures. They lived better than a lot of people, with heat, air conditioning, blankets, TV and homemade food.

Bonobos come from only one spot in the world: a tiny forest in the midst of the Congo River Basin near Kinshasa, where there's been so much war and corruption and death, such an active bushmeat trade putting their fleshy bones on the tables of European restaurants, that only a few hundred bonobos are still thought to still live there.

People would call on the phone wanting to know why we kept the apes in cages. Is that humane treatment? they would ask. Shouldn't they be living in the wild? It was my job to take these calls, usually one or two a week. It took me forever to learn what to say.

Julian taught me to use a calm voice and the correct terminology, and to try not to upset anybody. But the real answer was this: most of the apes at our lab were born into captivity. They ate hamburgers and were toilet-trained and watched "The Swiss Family Robinson" on video and went to bed at 6. If we were to turn them loose, or fly them back to Africa and leave them on the thin strip of Congo riverbank where they were supposed to have come from, they'd be jumped like tourists in a bad neighborhood.

The apes at our lab used specially designed symbols imprinted on a computer keyboard to communicate with the staff. If they wanted to go outside, they'd walk up to the computer, bolted down to a huge white plastic box in their enclosure, and press the key for outside, and the computer would say the word.

Once when I was slinking around looking for Soraya in the hallway, I heard her voice over a monitor. The voice came from her darkened office. I slunk against a wall and inched up to the door to get closer, to see what was happening, to see her. I started when I saw Julian leaning against the wall in her office, holding a video camera over his shoulder as he taped a research session in the apes' bedroom.

Faraji sat on a white Lexan cube, an ape chair that held him three feet up in the air. He had old-style headphones on, cracked brown plastic pillows covering each ear. He looked like an ape air-traffic controller. He sat, relaxed, his huge arms at his sides, and looked at the keyboard.

Soraya stood over against the gray cement-block wall. She had headphones on too, and spoke into a microphone. She was so beautiful. My cheeks and neck burned. I stared at her, then snuck looks at Julian to see if it looked like he noticed the way I looked at Soraya. I couldn't tell.

"Okay, Faraji, we're going to start again. Are you ready?" Soraya sang out. We all looked at her. Her voice filled the ape room and came into the office through the monitor, wrapping around us like a sheet. Back in the ape room, Faraji nodded gamely and turned his attention back to the keyboard.

I sneaked so many looks at Julian to see if he noticed my reaction that he could feel them, and he darted glances over his shoulder at me.

"What, Deb?" he said finally, irritated.

"What?" I pretended I hadn't been looking at him. I tried to giggle but was mortified.

"Why are you looking at me, Deb?"

"I'm…I'm not looking at you, Julian."

"Okay, well, stop not looking at me, Deb," he said, turning

back to the scene in the ape room, and pressed record again.

Used to be I'd stare at a man, he'd like it, I thought. When I was younger I let my blonde hair grow out long, curly, bushing out almost against light freckled skin, making me look super skinny and childlike. I cut it up to my shoulders when I had Chloe, gained the kind of weight that makes you look like you don't have a waist at all. Men stopped looking. They all treated me like a sister, sometimes like a pesky younger one who followed them around and asked too many questions. Marc was starting to do it too now – and he looked so much like me that people had actually mistaken him for my brother.

Of course that was why I floated toward dark Soraya, toward an unknowable woman, as I never had before. I think about it now and it's textbook psychology, but while it was happening it felt like stepping into a force field, sucked up by magnets, shoved to the ground.

I didn't realize Joie was in the ape room with Faraji, but now he rushed the window and jumped off the Lexan wall, his black ape feet slamming the thick plastic window with a BAM that made me jump and clutch my heart. He landed on the cement floor and did it again, falling onto his back and shaking his feet in the air, his hands clapping and his jaw hanging open in a pantomime of a laugh.

I learned, too, that our lab was a model for humane treatment of primates. Years ago, in other labs, chimpanzees were kept in windowless, white boxes and injected with AIDS, so that scientists could see what happened to chimpanzees injected with AIDS. Soraya helped to build our lab from scratch in the early 1980s to focus solely on cognitive research. All our faculty abided by the Great Ape Project agreement, stipulating basic rights for all chimpanzees, bonobos, gorillas and orangutans used for research, so that they'd be protected from biomedical experimentation. So none of the apes at our lab were ever kept in windowless boxes, and they were only ever injected with anything when they were sick and the vet came to take care of them. Their enclosures were made of Lexan, a two inch-thick clear plastic resin, and chain link, so much chain link that after a few weeks I felt like it surrounded me too.

The bonobos at our lab were: Faraji, at 25 the most gregarious, a charismatic star. He was 20 pounds overweight and related to every adult female ape at the lab, so he didn't have a girlfriend. When he was alone he humped his stuffed Elmo doll. Imena, 20, was an eternally pregnant diva, haranguing the staff for treats. Bonobos make love all the time and so while she usually got impregnated by Yashashiku, nicknamed Yi-ku, the 32 year-old retired Japanese circus ape, the staff couldn't ever really be sure. Yi-ku was thin, wiry and wily, not especially personable but calm and usually reasonable, a mensch.

Malika — "Mommy" — who had given birth to five babies now living with her in captivity at the lab, was wild-caught in the jungle outside Kinshasa when she was about eight. By that time she'd already adopted Faraji, whose mother put him out when he was an infant. Some versions of the same story held that Malika stole him — a few different stories were told about that time in the 70s and 80s, when ape language research really began to get going in a few select university research labs. Malika was the Southern University Primate Research facility's original bonobo subject.

Soraya and her students tried for years, with no success, to teach Malika to use the computer keyboard. Malika just sat there and kept pointing at her food bowl until they let her eat, but Faraji, then an infant playing in the cage behind her, heard every word and remembered all of it, using the keyboard and key utterances to communicate with staff ever since.

The adult apes were moody. They're big, black, hairy, can weigh up to 300 pounds and could easily beat the hell out of you if they wanted to. When Imena was heavily pregnant, she'd point her cracked, black fingers at the "blueberries" key on the computer keyboard several times a day, and refuse to deal with anyone until Soraya laid them at her feet. Sometimes Julian delivered the berries, sometimes Clara or Christine. But usually it had to be Soraya.

But the little ones are spritely and sweet. Joie, one of the youngest, had open greenish-brown eyes and soft, shiny fur that shone in the reflection of the overhead lights like a dog after a bath. They jump around like little black elves. The younger ones smile at visitors and hold out their hands for M&Ms.

…

One day after I'd been at the job a few weeks, Christine called me on the radio and said we needed to go on an errand. She'd be around in the lab's other SUV, a huge maroon Chevy Tahoe, in a few minutes, and I needed to bring cash.

It was raining lightly, the drops staining the blacktop and snaking back up in mist that reached to my knees. Christine rolled down the passenger side window as I walked up.

"It's burrito time," she called, brightly. "How much money do you have? Do you have like $50? We're going to need a lot of burritos."

I opened the door and stepped into the cab. It smelled like moldy leaves. The clouds made everything dark, so at first I didn't immediately make out the big rips in the plum-colored upholstery or the fact that the dashboard was listing, nearly completely yanked out on the passenger side, hanging by red and black wires. I reached for the seat belt and Christine shook her head. Joie had been in the vehicle the week before and had ripped them out.

"Welcome to the Apemobile," she said as she put her own

entire right side into action to shift the huge SUV into reverse. "Soraya isn't supposed to take the apes out in it, but guess what. She sneaks them out at every opportunity."

I just took in the smell and the sights.

"The apes? Ride around? In this car?"

Christine nodded and threw her whole right shoulder into drive, and we started moving forward slowly.

"Yup. At night, after I go home. We're not allowed to have them out of their enclosures. We used to do it all the time, just let them sit in the car while we went through the drive-thru, but then we took them to McDonald's once and somebody saw and freaked out. They got scared and called the cops. We got reported. So now if anybody was to, say, take Faraji out in the Tahoe during the day, I'd lose my job. So Soraya sneaks them out at night. She thinks we don't know."

I still wanted time to take all this in, and I tried not to look at the hanging dashboard for a minute. I was the one they'd call from downtown when they wanted to update the insurance or have a mechanic come out and maintain the vehicles. Nobody had said a word to me about apes riding around in the SUVs at night.

"I spent two hours cleaning out this goddamned vehicle last week, and it was in great shape. Soraya gets alone with the apes over the weekend and they take the whole fucking thing apart."

Christine looked at the road, chewing her lips a bit, having spat out the only negative she would really allow herself. I still didn't know what to say.

"We've been picked to go get tacos for everybody, lucky us," she went on. "Burritos, I mean, burritos. Everybody except Soraya."

"Where's Soraya?"

"I haven't seen Soraya for days, myself. She's on that weird diet. I'm sure you've heard all about that."

I told her I hadn't heard a word.

"She eats nothing but butter. Supposed to help her lose weight. She drinks orange juice and eats sticks of butter out of the wax paper. Only." She chuckled bitterly and looked out at the road.

I thought Christine was joking. I looked straight ahead, giggling, and I didn't say anything. She didn't say anything either. I couldn't believe the butter thing wasn't just a joke, a slur against Soraya.

"Butter. No. Really? Seriously? But she's not overweight."

"Whatever. We had a meeting in her office last week and she had a half stick of melting butter on her desk and she'd pick it up and eat off it every couple of minutes. Grossest thing I've ever seen, and the apes do a lot of disgusting stuff."

Now I couldn't think of a response.

"Anyway that's why you haven't seen her. She's probably been in the bathroom. It's like, she's God to this lab, she's Jesus. The apes won't make a move without her and the people are not far behind. Which makes it all the more crazy that she's such a nutjob," she took her eyes off the road for just a second to gauge my reaction. "I mean, right? Don't you think?"

I laughed a little, mumbled "yeah" or something and stared at the road ahead myself, afraid to take my eyes off it. I couldn't see a thing wrong with Soraya's mind. My only problem was that I didn't know her nearly as much as I wanted to. I wanted to be inside it, to think her thoughts, see this car and this road and this woman beside me driving just as she saw them, say what she'd say. I wanted to be with Soraya and I wanted to be Soraya. In the back of my head was that low, needling whine, that said Danger! What are you getting yourself into here?

Christine didn't notice. She was still chuckling to herself, focusing on the road, shaking her head.

"She's Jesus. She's an Iranian Jesus," she muttered.

So she's an Arab, I thought. That explains a lot, her dark hair and skin. Her deep, brown eyes. She was slim like a Persian cat, I thought. She smelled like spices. I clamped my mouth shut, afraid the words would come tumbling out and Christine would figure out everything I was thinking in a second.

On the way back she took a corner hard and I fell forward off the grimy Chevy bench, my left hand grasping a Taco Bell bag the size of my torso and the other reaching out to block my fall. My hand shoved through and behind a jagged rip in the dashboard and got tangled up in hot, greasy wiring.

"Oops. Sorry," she said.

When we got back, there were extra burritos. I waited until everyone had cleared out of the conference room and two bean burritos were sitting wrapped up in the box on the table, got a Coke out of the refrigerator and brought them back to Soraya's office.

She was sitting at her desk writing on a legal pad when I walked in. She had her feet propped up on a plastic crate under the desk, and next door in the ape room, Faraji and Imena laid on carpets and played lazily with Joie's younger brother Aya, who was only two and bouncing around like a kitten. Faraji laid stretched out, propped up on his arm, eating a banana. He looked over his shoulder and watched me walk in and put the food on Soraya's desk.

I was watching Faraji watch me, so I didn't immediately see Soraya look up. When I looked back she was watching me, smiling broadly. She took one of the burritos and unwrapped it.

"I didn't know you were going out for lunch. That's so thoughtful of you, Deb."

46

I just stared at her a minute. What about the whole butter thing? Christine had her all wrong.

Soraya laughed around a mouthful of burrito. "What?"

I sat down in the big leather chair that I was beginning to love. A few times during my first weeks there, when Soraya was out in the field or in one of the other buildings with Faraji and Imena, I'd come here in the middle of the day and sit and look out of the window, plug in Soraya's tape of Indestructible Beat of Soweto Volume One, look at her books, her notes. I didn't know if she knew, or not. It always felt okay, like she wouldn't mind.

Whenever I entered a room Soraya was in, she'd make sure to broadcast her smile at me, step back from the person she was talking to so that she would include me in their group, invite me over to talk. By the end of the first week, if I had a day where I didn't run into her in the hallway and get to talk for just a few minutes, it didn't feel right. She'd looked right at me across the desk just weeks ago and asked me, though not in so many words, to join her life, her family. Though that day I brought the burritos, I was still attempting to tell myself I was there because it was a good next move for my career, whatever I thought that was at the time. Not because I was starting to get a little obsessed.

I finished lunch and kept sitting there with Soraya, wanting to stay there all afternoon. She talked and I listened, stories about who in the ape family was angry with whom. Faraji and Malika had an alliance going against Imena, who was impetuous and angry, flailing shit at them because they wouldn't groom with her. The babies sensed the tension, Soraya said, and wouldn't go near Imena when she was so upset, and she felt even more ostracized, lashed out, got even more obnoxious.

It made me think of fighting with my brothers as a kid, of getting in trouble, so upset my head felt swollen. Then we'd all have to sit down to dinner together while I was still so upset, choking back broccoli at the family table, so self-conscious my arms felt six feet long and my hands the size of watermelons. I told Soraya about it.

"See, and you couldn't even throw shit at them. The bonobos have a much better way of dealing with things like that. They just throw it. They don't worry about being civilized. They're more human than we are, really."

Of course everyone has an animal side, hiding behind the scrim of our ordinary human sides, lurking around the corners. Dark, dirty, picking nits. You can't see a person's animal side until you know them for a really long time. Then you stumble up on their animal, their hairy, smelly ape, hunched over and angry. When my alarm goes off in the morning, it's my ape who turns it off, burying her hairy arms back under the covers and glowering at the outside world from under there. I want to be the meditative, dedicated me who set it the night before, but she's not the one in the bed and she never does wake up.

5

She found me.

The next day Soraya found me. The sex, the love, found me. Both. All.

I am not a woman who loves women. Usually. I am a married woman who loves men. Usually. But I loved Soraya somehow, and I was starting to feel a little more comfortable with that. I loved Chloe and Faraji and Marc and Soraya. I kept them separate during the day and meted out love to each one, according to their places in my life, when I could. Each of them took and wanted more, or less, or different, but there was work to do and I always had places to be. I had to pick up one and drop off another and work with one and sit with another while they were sick or worried, even just a little upset about something small, and there was never time, never any time to sort it out to make it what it needed to be with any of them. I did small things and it worked okay most days and none of them ever mentioned another. I gave the pieces of myself away, and for awhile it worked.

With Chloe it was easy when she talked to redirect her to

where I wanted her to be, to send her to Marc for the daily stuff and turn her back around to me for what I thought was the big love. I thought if I just stared into her big wide eyes and held her and didn't talk, this whole big mess that was who I suddenly loved wouldn't matter so much. Chloe had to know I loved her, I thought. She was still so little I was afraid she might forget about me once I dropped her off at school in the mornings and headed for the lab. Marc made her bottles and picked her up when I worked late and watched PBS Kids and made sure there were enough Big Kid diapers in the bag she took every day to school.

Marc himself seemed so institutional to me at the time, so strong and silent he'd faded completely into the background. He'd become Dad to me, moved into a role about equal to Chloe's teachers, only around to keep me in line and help me while I worked so much and so hard. He was allowed to chide me but not too much; if he got mean or sarcastic I cut him out. I removed him from my orbit. If Chloe's teachers faded into the background on nights and weekends when I didn't need them, so did Marc. So did Marc. And he didn't say anything about it, so I thought it was probably okay.

We took Chloe back and forth to school and bought diapers and packed up snacks. We dealt with teachers and read all those little daily reports of when she ate, how long she slept, her mood, her accomplishments, her little life recorded on half-sheets of paper every day. Every morning we looked at the sheet from the day before, wondering whether to throw it away or save it forever. There was only ever about three minutes to decide. Is there time to wipe the oatmeal off the goddammned thing and go put it away before we have to get in the car? Is it better to just pitch it and wash out the little plastic takeout container Marc had put her strawberries in and pack up her lunch for today, her carrots and cut-up hot dogs and pineapple chunks in their cute little cans, pack it all up and hope she did something unbelievable again that her teachers would record again on today's half-sheet of paper? If it didn't get ruined by the leftover food in the bag, then if we were super-careful we could save it, and put it in the one of the four memory books Marc's mother had bought us and prove that we loved her, we loved her so, so, so much.

It was the only real care I gave Chloe during that time. Those few minutes in the morning before I left for the lab, going through her little baby backpack, breathing in the sweet astringent plastic that smelled like fruit candy, reading the notes on her life. Pretending I'd been there, pretending that it was fine that I hadn't been, just fine. Marc would be with her at night. They'd process her day together. I would get there when I could. It would be fine.

Now when I think of what happened between Soraya and me, I think of backpacks and cans of fruit and sandwich bags with blue and green interlocking tops, of spilled-milk blotches on the little papers that are all I have of Chloe as she was then. I was open to Soraya, waiting for her and wanting her, but in my mind my back is to the room and my whole attention is on the kitchen countertop, on 3-ounce cans of pineapples and pears, tiny ravoli in microwavable bowls, little plastic forks and folded paper towels and notes back to teachers on half-slips of paper. The thought of Soraya's breath in my ear makes me think of a black-and-white drawing of a teddy bear in the corner of one of those daily teacher reports. On the floor with the bear are ABC blocks and a notation in blue pen of the exact time Chloe fell asleep for her nap and that she didn't finish her lunch that day, and on my chest are Soraya's fingernail scratches where she dug like she was climbing me, healed now but I can still feel where they were, like we were falling and she grabbed on and held us both up. Because that's what happened. That's what happened.

When I would take my lunch and sit by the chain link at the lab and talk with the apes, they'd often make a small halfhearted gesture for my hand, as if to say they'd hold it but for the fencing. And when they wanted to show each other something, one of them would come over and take the other's hand. If Faraji wanted an audience with Imena or Malika he would come to get them. He'd swing over to them and reach for the hand closest to him. Sometimes he'd make high-pitched, chirping come-hither noises, almost like a bird. Sometimes he was silent. Their hands would interlock like teenagers', his big muscled arm and her long, stringy one, covered with long black shiny hair. Imena would do it too, big, loud Imena, just go over to Joie if she wanted him and reach for him. If he was busy playing and she wanted him to eat, she'd come and get him that way.

That was how Soraya came to get me. It was a Wednesday, close to seven, I was getting ready to leave. She came wordlessly, looking not at my face but my hands, coffee-colored skin where Marc was light, smiling like a child. Our cars were the only ones left in the lot. All the lights were still on in the building and I'd been packing up slowly, wondering what she was up to.

She led me back through the hallways and past the faculty and student offices. We hugged the walls because she turned out all the lights as she went. I thought she had something to show me in the back but was being efficient, doing her nighttime duties, making sure the lights were out. Soon it was totally dark inside, and she led me slowly through the big conference room, lit only from the outside by the lights of the parking lot.

By the time we reached the far hallway in the back of the building by her office, my eyes had already adjusted to the lack of light. I could see through the window to the apes' bedrooms that they were already in bed, yellow industrial nightlights glowing near the gates to the cages they slept in. We crept though and

Soraya gripped my hand. What little light was there disappeared into her hair. She still hadn't said anything to me.

Then we were at the back door, the one leading outside and to the woods. We went straight through it. Soraya's keys jangled against her back pocket. She must have had 30 of them, on a big silver ring the size of a man's hand. A big yellowish outdoor light glowed under a ripped plastic casing near the door. Bugs flew around it and it gave off a glow that made our skin look greenish and our lips and eyes purple. But Soraya kept going out to the path leading through the woods where it was darker, still so early evening that the moon hadn't fully risen yet. I asked her what she was taking me to see. She looked down at her feet to find where the path started and just pulled on my hand, sending an electric jolt that traveled up through the muscles in my arm and settled in my chest with something heavy and hard like fear.

We trudged up the path, holding hands. I saw finally that we were heading for the clearing where they took Faraji for picnics. But Soraya stopped short of going into the open area and turned sharply toward a huge oak at the edge of the woods. Our arms, still interlaced, were closer now and more taught as she guided me to the tree. I could smell her, a scent like sun and lavender, cinnamon, pears maybe. I stumbled a little, behind her, and steadied myself with a hand on her back, my nose inches from her chocolate hair. It was exhilarating, being outside at night like a kid on Halloween, creeping over dry leaves and ducking under tree branches in the dark, all the rules suspended at least until the sun comes up.

Then she swung me around, my back up against the oak, her face inches from mine. I remember I didn't feel afraid exactly, that I looked into her eyes and felt ready for whatever she would do. But the cold hardness in my chest was spreading, almost knocking out my breath. I know I wanted to stay there with her, but I felt myself draining out, moving away, gasping for air. Before I knew it I was fighting her, kicking with limbs that were going numb, and she held me there and whispered to me like mother to child.

"Sshh, stop," she said, melodic. "Don't struggle."

I shook my head to clear it. "I don't want to," I said, looking down at the dried leaves, shaking now, wagging my head from side to side, the only control I felt I had left over my body. My heart beat so hard in my ears I could hardly hear myself. "Leave, I mean. I don't want to leave. But I can't….my body wants to run and stay at the same time. I don't know what's happening."

She stepped back, still holding me there lightly, and we looked at each other. It was like seeing another self. Same sex, same height, same clothes and boots tracked through the same mud, bodies and thoughts and lives almost identical. She took her index finger and put it on my forehead, traced it lightly down my nose, over my lips and chin.

"That's just the fight or flight response. You've heard of that, right? You're in a dangerous situation," she said, her eyes flashing, her voice breathy. "You want to be here with me and you don't, at the same time. Your heart is beating out of control. It's all you can do to stand up right now. Is that about right?"

I nodded. I didn't feel like I could speak. The moon was climbing, low in the sky just over the tops of the trees. It shone on her hair and lit up the side of her face, so beautiful.

"You can overcome it, Deb. Just want to be here with me. Just want it. That's all. That's all you have to do." Melodic, sing-songy, like we'd been here before together, like we'd rehearsed it. It did feel a bit like the natural curve to a role I'd taken months ago, sitting with her in her office, wanting to be near her, to hear her talk, to watch her. I'd put out of my mind what all those thoughts really meant, what it all wanted to add up to, never dared think I actually wanted to be with someone other than Marc and Chloe before I met her. Now here I was and she was all I wanted. We were in the woods together and Soraya was kissing me, her hands on me, in me, my body fluctuating between numb torpor and hot sparks, my toes moving like to get ready to run, my heels grinding into the dirt to stay there forever.

6

She might get the message,
and she might not.

Faraji and Imena spent the next day lounging around while the little ones climbed all over them, playing and pulling their hair, asking for M&Ms. Then the babies scampered off together, rolling and tumbling, bouncing off the enclosure walls and landing, splayed out on the floor, like black, leggy kittens. Soraya and I sat cross-legged in front of them on the floor, watching them through the chain link.

I'd barely slept the night before, lying there in the dark thinking about her, waiting for it to be light so I could get back to the lab. I'd forgotten to get myself breakfast but I remembered a banana for Faraji on my way out the door. Then, bleary-eyed and freaked out, I drove in and went straight from my car to where I knew she'd be, not bothering even to set my things down in my office. I found her there in front of the enclosure, making notes with a pen and a legal pad. She smiled as I came up and sat down next to her but she said nothing.

Faraji sauntered gracefully over and hooked two long, black fingers out through the chain link. Then he leaned back and swung there a little. I asked him if he wanted the banana and he nodded, more quickly than you would think anyone could move a head that big, showing his big pink gums in a huge, toothy grin.

Imena just lay there, hugely pregnant. I handed the banana to Faraji through the fencing and Imena slowly leveled her head to look over at me, clear out of her world at the other side of the chain link like an idiot. I thought she could probably tell I hadn't thought to bring anything for her, and anyway she was tired. She looked at us like she would really have preferred we just take the babies somewhere else so she could relax in peace.

I sat cross-legged next to Soraya, a feeling in my chest that I couldn't catch my breath, no food in my stomach since lunch the day before, running on nervous energy that couldn't last, waiting for an inevitable crash. I remembered being pregnant with Chloe, needing protein and baked goods every half hour just so that we could both survive. Now I didn't think I could ever face food again.

I had no words for what I felt for Soraya then. I'd only met her weeks before. I was consumed by not knowing what, if anything, she felt for me. The night before, I'd felt singular, so special, as if she and I were the only two people under the sky. Now I was sitting next to her on the floor like an employee or a student. I needed so much more information, questions flying around my head like crackles off a sparkler: Does she want me or does she do that with everyone? Is this love or some crazy rite she goes through with all the new people? I thought of Julian, of Christine, who didn't seem to have much of a rich connection with her, and of Uba. I wondered what she thought of Uba. She hadn't said anything to me about any of them. But now I was so painfully aware that she also hadn't said anything to me about me. The night before felt like an invitation, but she never said to what. I'd thought we might spend the next day talking about it. Now here I was and she wasn't talking at all.

Well, she talked a little.

"So did you reach those people from London?" she asked that morning, out of the blue.

"No…what people?" I tried to keep my voice light, but I wanted to cry.

"BBC, I think – I got a message they wanted to come film here."

My face was hot and I stared at the ground, sullen, confused like back when I was a teenager. I just shrugged.

"They didn't call me," I frowned.

Of course they didn't call me. They didn't know to call me. She was the famous one, she was the one they'd naturally try to reach. She might get the message and she might not. It was my job to find out who they were and what they wanted, and then call them back and tell them why they couldn't come. But being insolent was the only way I could think of to hurt her, so I was insolent. I blew it off.

So we just sat there together for a little while, her watching the apes and me watching her, and none of my questions would come and she didn't say a word. After a few minutes all my questions formed into a big ball of goo in my stomach in the place where I usually put food. Watching Faraji eat the banana made my gut wrench. I put both my hands over my stomach and leaned forward, staring at the concrete floor, knowing only that she was not noticing it. I thought she must be able to feel my nervous, sick energy, that any second she'd turn to me and say we needed to talk about last night. But she didn't. She'd just blown my world up and now she was unavailable.

I sat there until I couldn't sit there anymore. Then I got up and went back to my office without having said another word to her.

…

I had thought we were ready for escapes. I guess we were, but only in a theoretical way. Sometimes while I ate lunch with my colleagues in the conference room, we'd plot out our individual escape plans. For instance, what would we do if the apes broke out of their enclosures in the back of the building and ran around to the front, blocking the flight to our cars? I hadn't told anyone yet about my own personal plan, which was to go into my office, lock the door and call 911. Then I'd just stay there until help arrived.

When I finally did tell Christine this one day at lunch, she just laughed. She put down her sandwich and led me from the conference room, where we were all eating together, to stand in front of my office door. Then she pointed to the top of the door, showing me that it didn't quite meet the ceiling. In fact, there was a good ten inches of clearance up there. Plenty of room for our conversations to float out and be heard pretty clearly by Ardelle at the reception desk. Plenty of room for rogue apes, if they were really bent on mauling you, to scale the wall and vault over the top.

"So Faraji just…" she ran back to in front of Ardelle's desk and mimed getting up on top of it, "he just jumps up here, no problem, and he can get to you in about two minutes."

She reassured me then, in her bleach-eaten jeans and faded green Yosemite t-shirt, her long blonde hair held back in an orange cotton scrunchie.

"Don't worry, though," she said, actually patting my hand. "I've got a gun."

I stared at her, speechless.

"And permits," she said. "We all do."

Also, she told me, tasers, ketamine, and six-foot pointed sticks. And some kind of nasty potion to rub on the tips.

"All of you have guns?" I looked around at them.

"No," Clara/Kalala said low and soft, shaking her head and looking down at her sweatpanted legs, crossed one over the other, her sandwich in her lap. "I do not have a gun. Uba does not have a gun."

Christine shrugged.

"Most of us do. For security, Deb." And the subject was dropped there, but then after lunch Christine walked me back to my office. It was part of my responsibility to help her keep up with the paperwork we needed to keep all the drugs around. I hadn't known about guns, though, or tasers. She opened the bottom drawer of my desk. They hadn't ever gotten around to cleaning it out since my predecessor, the previous business manager, couldn't hack it and left after three months. Inside was a shiny black taser, round and gleaming like a giant tick, tucked at the ready in the back. It sat on top of its Official Taser Instruction Booklet, still taped shut with a sticker seal.

And anyway, you couldn't call 911. A few months before I started at the lab, Christine was cleaning Faraji's cage one day, and he grabbed her arm through the chain-link fence and bit off three of the fingers on her right hand. The maintenance man was driving by in his golf cart, and the first thing he did was call 911 on his cell phone. The ambulance came three minutes later. The next day Soraya spent six hours defending the research protocol in an emergency meeting with the university's vice president while

50 or 60 animal rights activists staged a sit-in outside the lab gates.

The problem with 911 was that the calls went out over the police scanners to every cop and hobbyist in the Atlanta metro area. In the days after Faraji attacked Christine, cop cars started driving by slowly, peering through the woods, trying to see the crazy human-eating apes. All that summer, scanner hobbyist layabouts who saw staff members in their lab t-shirts waiting in line to buy chow and ape treats at the grocery store would be all over them, wanting to know what they did in the woods with the apes. They usually called the apes monkeys, though.

That attack had happened nearly three months ago, but people still occasionally happened by. One day I answered the main phone line to intercept a call from the front gate, where two guys were laughing over the roar of some souped-up car.

"Yo!" one of them called into the receiver. "Where da monkeys at?"

They didn't know the passcode, so they couldn't get in and they drove away. Or at least they didn't try to buzz in again. A pack of wild dogs ran together over the lab's 55-acre expanse, yes, amazingly, wild dogs in metro Atlanta, who chased another lab assistant from the main road back to the ape buildings one day, snarling and baring crusty, yellow fangs. I never saw them myself, but people said they greeted anybody who left their car at the gate and try to walk in.

Now it was May, and Christine still sported three bandaged half-fingers on her right hand. I'd been afraid to ask about it that first day, but she told me the whole story soon enough. Now, on request, she would show you where her blonde waves were still red at the roots where Faraji had tried to pull it out.

I found out that, if you work more than an hour with caretakers of chimpanzees and bonobos, you'll notice that even the most successful of them are missing digits. When we all sat around the big conference table for lab events, five different staff members including Soraya would hold up their half-eaten fingers and tell their stories. Christine was missing two and still worked with apes every day. She told us she wasn't afraid of apes, but now had an irrational fear of garbage disposals based on her ape attack. I guess it's hard to admit you're afraid of something if you have to show up at work and look it in the face every day.

Sometimes the bitten people can tell you why they think it happened, things they'd felt they'd done to make the apes mad. Maybe Christine didn't let Faraji go outside one day because they needed to finish a research trial, or told him no he couldn't have burritos, only salad, because he was overweight. One of Soraya's graduate students left the lab after losing the middle finger of his right hand from the knuckle up. He'd sworn it all happened because Faraji was pissed off that a visiting woman scientist was "being mean" and trying to upstage Soraya.

But most often people got bitten and had no real idea why. When they signed up to work with apes, they joined a secret society of missing-digit people.

But I'd never been close enough to be bitten, and until that ice cream day, none of the apes had gotten out of their enclosures during my time there. Escapes had only really happened once or twice in the lab's 25-year tenure. One day Christine told me the worst story, of an escape that had happened two years earlier. Lincoln and Yeli, two adult male chimpanzees who'd since been removed to the zoo, had escaped from their outdoor chain-link cages attached to the back of the Main Building on a weeknight around 9 p.m. All the caretakers checked each other's locks before going home for the night, but someone must have missed one, Christine said. The apes ran around outside like angry drunks, chasing the dogs around, ripping low-hanging branches from the trees. They let themselves in through the lab's open front doors.

No one was there but the cleaning people, a man and a woman, elderly part-timers. The apes pulled them away from their mopping, bit them and chased them all over the conference room. The woman got a big gash on her leg when she tripped over a chair. Lincoln broke the man's arm and bit off the top half of the middle finger of his right hand.

The woman called up and quit a few days later. Everyone said the man got an undisclosed settlement from the university and was asked very politely not to sue. When they threw a 25th anniversary party for the lab and invited him along with lots of other former employees, he didn't show up.

Ardelle started as the lab's receptionist a couple of weeks after I did. When she came out to the lab for her job interview, she was 15 minutes late. She ran from the parking lot to the main building like she was leaving a crime scene. Dressed in a beautiful white suit and heels, her hair in an understated up-do, she hugged her white leather purse so tightly to her chest she needed help to open the front door. She sat down at the conference table with bugged-out eyes darting all over the room.

I started asking her questions and she set her purse down and cracked up laughing. She apologized for being late, wiped tears from her eyes, and said it had taken her 20 minutes to drive a mile and a half from the main road because she drove three miles an hour and kept thinking an ape was going to jump out of the woods at her.

"Oh, Lord," she laughed. "Where am I? What is this?"

Now it was me shrugging, trying to sound like Christine, blithe and joking.

"Once you know the apes, they don't scare you that much anymore," I said. "Maybe think of them as big obnoxious teenagers who don't really talk?"

She just chuckled, very low, starting to relax a bit but not letting her guard down. I wondered if she ever would, and why I'd done it so quickly, so thoughtlessly.

"I'm pretty sure that's not going to happen, Miss Deb," she said. But she was smiling, so I took it as a sign she was ready to come on board.

...

Christine and I were eating ice cream in my office the day the ape got out. We were both supposed to be doing something else — she should have been cleaning cages and it had occurred to me I should look into that BBC film crew thing that Soraya mentioned the week before, maybe go snoop around her desk and try to find the phone message slip. But it was heavy and hot out, and we couldn't imagine actually working that afternoon.

Soraya and I had been together about two weeks before, and I hadn't been able to find five minutes to talk to her since. She was never around. We communicated mostly via email and very short phone calls. We never discussed what had happened. I was getting used to feeling like I couldn't breathe. I lost eight pounds. Marc could tell something was up but I never told him what. Every day she played on my mind, my whole body, a cancer that had been diagnosed but not yet treated.

Green pollen mixed with the dirt and coated all the cars in the lab's parking lot, crusting on the big magnolia leaves and hugging the skins of the pines. Heat wrapped around your t-shirt and climbed up your neck when you walked outside, but it was dark and cool in my office. If you turned out the lights and looked out the window into the woods around the parking lot, it was like a green, leafy movie.

Christine had coffee ice cream with chocolate sauce. It made her happy and hoppy, and she'd soon be spraying bleach from a bucket in the cages and hosing them down with a little spring in her step.

Then Julian blurted out over the radio that an ape was out.

Christine and I looked at each other, our eyes wide. Then she just picked up her radio and walked out. It was all very quiet.

I walked out of my office and sat down in the chair next to Ardelle's desk. We wordlessly found our radios and turned the volume dials as high as they would go. We listened through the still and quiet for sounds of something breaking. We paced the floor. I wouldn't let her call 911.

Then came Kalala/Clara's staccato bursts over the radio.

"It's Yi-ku. I can see him. He's gotten out of the inner enclosure…he's in the outer one though, and he seems to want to leave… but I'm blocking the exit, kind of, I'm leaning against the gate. So I'll need some backup, please."

Christine was already walking around to the back, and she calmly radioed Kalala/Clara that she'd be right there.

Ardelle and I passed a tense 20 minutes, still not knowing what to do with ourselves. I walked back into my office and decided I should try to proceed with my work normally, so I pulled out the vet supply catalog and started to order ape chow. That felt completely ridiculous.

Apparently Christine had gone out to the enclosure and approached from the outside, because when she used the radio to talk to Clara we could hear crickets in the background.

She didn't say a whole lot over the radio once she got up close to the situation. Ardelle and I sat in the silence and looked at each other. Nobody else went back to help because they didn't want to freak out Yi-ku. So they came up to the front desk and hung out, drinking coffee made that morning or water from the cooler in the hall. Julian leaned on Ardelle's desk, listening for radio missives with us. We were afraid to go outside and we didn't want to go back to our desks. We tried not to seem like we didn't know what to do.

Another ten minutes of nothing passed, and then a blast of static came over one of the radios. It must have come from Kalala/Clara or Christine with the radio in their pockets, leaning against something and inadvertently pressing the talk button. In the silence it sounded like a shot.

"Jesus Christ!" Julian shouted, pacing. His body cut through the lab's stale air in jeans and a blue 25th anniversary lab t-shirt. His hand flew to the back of his neck. He'd donated a long black ponytail to Locks of Love the week before, and he kept stroking the short curls still left there, feeling for lost hair like a ghost limb.

"Okay, Clara, now back up just a little," Christine finally said over the radio. Then over the next two minutes: "Yeah…. okay. That'll work. Good man, Yi-Ku….No, just stay there for a minute…He wants to come in, I think…Yi-ku wants to do the right thing."

"I sure as hell hope so," Ardelle said under her breath. Ardelle in a lovely blue cotton dress, Ardelle who always wore a silver cross around her neck.

I stared out the window for five more minutes until Christine strode purposefully around and in through the front door. Yi-ku had seemed to be thinking about going for a walk near the river; she said he stared at it for a solid half hour. In the end, though, he just moved quietly back into the inner enclosure and went for his full food bowl, like that had been his idea the whole time.

7

She is very heavy.

One night about a week later, I found myself kneeling in the back of a state of Georgia van. It was completely dark and hot as the inside of a drier. The van beeped and lurched as it backed up to the hospital loading dock. Not the Central Receiving dock, where the medicine and supplies come in, but the smaller one hospital staff use for smoke breaks, the badly lit one, in the back, by the dumpster.

Our van was nicknamed Turtle. The van had to have a nickname, for some reason. I think if there had been two vans, we would have communicated via radio between the vans using our van nicknames, but that night there was only Turtle.

Six of us were crammed inside. Soraya drove, staring straight ahead, not talking to any of us, her skinny arms wrapped around the van's steering wheel. The rest of us squeezed in on the floor in the back of the van, arranged around Imena, who was knocked out on ketamine and strapped down to a stretcher.

Christine sat on Imena's right side, gripping the edge of a rough, green swatch of outdoor carpeting used as a blanket. Uba held the left side down and I knelt at the ape's feet, my back against the van's back doors, my chunky heels cutting into the backs of my thighs, staring at Imena's hairy black toes. Julian was on my left. He'd wrapped the blanket around Imena like a rope around a captive, as if it would hold her down if she woke up and broke out of her straps.

We all knew the blanket was mainly for us to more secure about the whole thing. If Imena woke up, that blanket wouldn't have helped us at all.

Julian got out a white mask that looked like the Hannibal Lechter one from the movie "Silence of the Lambs," but longer, stretched out — like how it would look it if you melted the plastic with a blow drier and pulled down on the chin and up on the forehead. It was two feet long and looked totally freakish even before Julian got it anywhere near Imena.

He told us that we'd put the mask on the ape as soon as we got to the hospital and cover her whole body with a sheet. That way we would have a good shot at whisking her through the hallways and straight into the MRI machine without anybody seeing her.

We hardly spoke the whole way to the hospital. We all stared at fixed points in the van: the muddy, black rubber floor mats, the dirty, green ape carpet, the brown vinyl covers of the driver's-side seat, smeared with what everybody hoped was bean burrito. When we did talk, we tended to whisper and giggle and then stared back down at the floor of the van.

The van's suspension was shot so every bump on the road felt like being thrown into a dumpster. After a pothole I grabbed my lower back and winced, muttered "damn!" under my breath, and looked around at the rest of them, in their comfy jeans and t-shirts. I still had a suit on. Julian squinted at me in the dark, calling me out.

"What are you wearing?" he sneered at me. "Why are you in heels?"

"I had a meeting downtown today. Nobody told me I was going to have to come tonight," I whined back.

Actually, I had been completely excited to go. I'd been heading out to the parking lot when I noticed the van parked next to my car, Uba and Julian taking the seats out of the back. I asked what they were doing and they looked at me greedily.

"I didn't think you were still here. We're getting the van ready to take Imena to Emory Hospital for her MRI," Julian said. He set a seat down on the ground and straightened back up. He looked at me like he was starving and I was a sandwich.

"We really need your help. The students were supposed to come and help us get her into the machine and everything but there was a big fight today. Soraya really pissed them off, so they left. Can you come?"

"How am I supposed to help you get Imena into an MRI machine?" I asked him. "How do you even do that?"

"It's not a problem," Uba said as he walked up behind me and set another seat on the ground. "She'll be unconscious and strapped down on a stretcher the whole time. We just need extra hands to get her out of the van and up to the MRI room. She is very heavy."

I'd started to very quietly hate and fear Uba. A few days before, I'd noticed I never saw Uba and Soraya in the same room together. Every time he said her name in a meeting in the conference room it sounded like he said it with such love. I had no idea how to find out whether it was true, and my after-lunch walks, when I skulked around the lab grounds trying to make people think I was just trying to get my exercise, I was secretly looking for them in empty offices, in lesser-used buildings, in the woods. I never found them. My jealousy was eating me. Now as he walked up behind me, the little hairs from my neck all the way down my back stood up in alarm and I instantly wanted to throw up.

Marc was probably making our dinner at home right now. He'd told Chloe he was making her favorite meatloaf, said it to her while I was in earshot because he wasn't really talking much to me anymore, and it made me want to spit up my breakfast.

I'd worked late every night this week and last. I thought back to that morning, how I'd stared at his back while he washed the dishes, my bag on my shoulder and my keys in my hand. He's skinny, I thought, wondering why I'd never noticed before. His shoulder blades stuck out through his t-shirt. In a minute he'd shower and head for his job at the mall. I never said it out loud, but in my head it ran like a sing-song: his job at the mall. His job at the mall. Like he was 15 and I was a snobby bitch teenager he was trying to date.

A good wife would put her keys down and go to him, put her arms around him, tell him she was sorry her job was consuming her, sorry for so many things she couldn't tell him about. Bury her head in his bony neck and try to come back to her family. But I couldn't envision myself actually doing any of those things, saying any of those things. So I went to work, thinking it would be a good idea to show up for his dinner and pretend for one night that things were normal. Now I wasn't going to make it.

"When do we go?" I asked Julian.

"Not for awhile," Julian said. "Not til about 10. We can't go until it gets really quiet at the hospital and they're not using the MRI. We need it for a couple of hours, when there aren't any humans around. Any patients see Imena, they're liable to freak right out. So we kind of have to do it in the dead of night, and we have to be kind of sneaky about it."

70

So I could have gone home for dinner and come back later. But I didn't. I had some work to catch up on anyway, and there was always the chance that Soraya might have a few minutes to talk to me, and I wasn't about to pass that up. Marc didn't answer the phone when I called to let him know.

I sat in my office for three hours, my ears pricking up at every sound, afraid to go to her and willing her to come to me. We hadn't had any substantive communication in the weeks that had crawled by since we went out into the woods together. That next day I'd felt like I'd been punched in the stomach, like I'd eaten bad fish. That gave way to anger, red rage that I saw all day, hanging there right in front of my eyes. I walked around mentally composing what I'd say to her when I saw her in the hallway, but I never saw her there.

Then I started to feel what I wanted to say to her in my body. So much time had gone by that I began to think words wouldn't work, that I'd need to walk up to her and grab her, pin her arms to her and spin her around to face me, to overpower her, to force her to see me. *Then* I'd speak to her. *Then* I could ask her what we were supposed to mean to each other now, what I was supposed to do.

It felt like bits of me were stretched out all over Atlanta, at home with Chloe, at my desk at the lab, in the woods with her. I didn't know where my body was in space anymore, and I knew I'd need to gather up all the parts to summon the force I'd need to say even one word to her now. I'd sit at my desk and flex my arm muscles, curl my hands into fists and stretch my fingers out again, staring at them, willing her to come and get me again, and she just never did.

I didn't see her that night until she stalked past my office a few minutes after 10, on her way out the front door, angrily tossing the van keys. I stood up to run after her, and that's when I remembered I was still wearing the pumps I'd put on for my meeting downtown that morning. I clunked after Soraya but she was walking too fast, and I never caught up before she writhed into the driver's seat and slammed the door shut. I walked around to the back of the van, sat on the bumper at its open back doors and waited for Julian and Uba to load Imena in, or for Soraya to realize I was there and come around and talk to me, something.

Now the Turtle van was almost to the hospital and Julian was giving me shit about my shoes.

"I'm sorry," Julian said. "I'm tense. It's just that everything has to go perfectly or we waste all kinds of money we paid Emory to use the MRI. Soraya spent the whole day railing about how she doesn't want to do it and then pissed off both the students who were supposed to help," he glared up toward her in the driver's seat.

We could feel Soraya parking the van then. I couldn't tell if she could hear us or not, but it felt like she was jerking it back and forth so that we'd fall all over Imena.

Julian started in on me again. "Anyway, why are you whispering?"

"I don't know. Because *you're* whispering. Because I don't want to wake Imena up."

"She is so not waking up," Julian whispered. "She might not wake up till next week."

Uba, black and bald, so big he seemed to take up the whole left side of the van, wore a brown t-shirt in the dark. I could only really see him if he spoke and the light from the street shone off his teeth. He used some kind of essential oil that smelled like lemon and wood smoke. I felt it move through the air as he swiveled his big head around to stare at Julian.

"Next week?" He said quietly. "Why?"

"Wait a minute," Christine snapped from across Imena's body,

72

making us all stop and stare back at her. "How much did you give her?"

"Ten megs of ketamine," Julian shrugged. "That's standard."

It meant nothing to me, but Christine's eyes got a little wider. No one said anything.

"What?" Julian looked around at us. "I told you guys. 10 megs is standard. We want to take chances here?"

Now Uba held up the white plastic Hannibal mask. Christine gently grasped Imena's head and held it still while Uba strapped it on. The mask made the ape look unbelievably scary, like a dead Bigfoot in the dark.

Now it was time to back out of the van and take her in. They'd told me when I started that heavy lifting was a part of the job. "Ability to lift a minimum of 50 lbs" was written right there on the list of requirements on all our job descriptions. But I'd thought they were talking about lifting big bags of ape chow, not actual apes. My stomach muscles were still weak from a c-section when Chloe was born, and at home I could barely pick up the dog.

"Anyway, let's go," Julian said. "Let's go. On three."

"Light as a feather, stiff as a board," Christine whispered.

Julian stopped and stared at her.

"Sorry? What?"

She shook her head, clearing it.

"What's that thing we used to do? Light as a feather, stiff as a board," she said, staring at Imena's head in the mask. Her hair was tied back under a baseball cap, but a couple of strands hung in her eyes as she stared at Imena.

"It's a levitation game I played at a slumber party once when I was a kid," she explained. "Everybody gathers around someone lying on the floor, and they can lift her up six feet in the air using only two fingers of each hand."

Julian blinked at her.

"Well sure," he said. "That's called a gravity antenna. You need at least five people and you can't do it unless you stack your hands on the person's head first. I played it too. As a kid….now could we please get this ape out of this van?"

"Gravity what?" Uba seemed to be giggling, or grimacing, hard to tell given the lack of light. I stared at my left hand. It would be so easy to let it slip off where I was holding the stretcher and slap him. In the dark I fantasized making it look like an accident. I'd turned him into my enemy and he didn't even know it. He would know it if I slapped him, though. If he wasn't such a gentle guy he could probably crush me under his foot like an empty cardboard box.

"As I was saying," Julian said, and I could nearly hear him rolling his eyes, "on three."

I climbed out of the van backwards, grunting, and then stood at the open back door, sticking both hands under Imena's stretcher to guide her out. This would be a good way to lose a finger. Suddenly two green-clad hospital guys appeared in the parking lot and wheeled a gurney up to the back of the van, and I had to jump out of their way in my heels. Moths hovered everywhere in the fluorescent floodlight, landing brown and papery on her sheet. I stood back as they wheeled her up to the base of the loading dock.

Uba stopped and looked toward the front of the van. That's when I realized Soraya was still sitting in the driver's seat. She didn't help us get Imena out and she hadn't said a word to anyone since before the Turtle van took off from the lab. Uba glided silently in his sneakers across the wet black of the parking lot. He went up to her at the driver's side window, hooking his arm inside the door and puts his face up next to hers. Christine saw me watching them.

"She didn't want to do this," she whispered to me.

"Why not?" I asked her. I wasn't sure exactly what she meant so I figured I might as well play dumb and learn something.

"Lots of reasons," Christine said. "I don't know…maybe because it might actually tell us something concrete. Maybe because we might someday, accidentally, publish something good."

The heavy hospital door squeaked open behind us. Soraya and Uba were huddled, their faces close together. I started going up to the van. Uba looked back over his big shoulder at me, startled. He broke away then and started back toward the stretcher.

"Come on Deb, let's go get her in there," he said, trying to pull me with his voice.

I closed my eyes as I passed him and kept walking up to the van.

Soraya wiped her eyes as I got up to her. She stared out over the steering wheel.

"What's wrong?" I asked her.

"How can you even ask me that?" she snapped back. "Everything. They drugged up Imena! They're going to put her in some huge machine. I hate it for her. It's not right!"

My hand was on the driver's side window. It started to float, on its own power, on the wet wind, toward her face. I had no power stop it. She didn't notice. She started beating lightly on the steering wheel.

"I had nothing to do with this. It's not my project," she said, as if she were talking to someone sitting between her and the windshield. "But we need the money, Julian says. Screw him. It's not right." She stared straight ahead.

I put my hand on her arm. She left both her hands on the steering wheel and turned to look into my face.

"Deb. Let's *go*," Julian called from the landing.

They had Imena up the steps and inside the door. Christine held it open. I skipped-clicked in my inappropriate shoes back across the parking lot and up through the door, and we wheeled Imena down the hallway and into a big shiny stainless-steel elevator. Nobody talked. We all stared at the floor and moved as quickly as possible.

Then the elevator opened and an old guy was standing there. A patient in a robe and slippers. He looked from our faces to the long black hair sticking out from under the sheet. His eyes got wide and he opened his mouth but didn't speak. Julian yanked the stretcher out of the elevator, speeding around and past him, shoving Imena up against the right side of the hallway.

We all gathered around her stretcher, wheeling her through the hospital, willing the gurney's wheels to stop their *squeak, squeak, squeak,* whipping around the corners as quickly as we could, constantly staring at the floor.

One more tight curve to the right and we were at the MRI room, where a bearded medical resident-looking guy let us in. He held open the door for us, nervous, looking both ways back out through the hall like he was sneaking in hookers. We wheeled Imena past him and lined her up next to the MRI machine, and took our places around her. I was on the side this time, looking at the machine's hard white bed and worrying about what would happen to my fingers if they got caught underneath Imena.

Then there was a *ring, ring* sound. We all looked around. Nobody knew where it was coming from. I looked toward the little MRI control room over in the corner, where we'd all gather once the ape was loaded into the machine. RING RING. We all looked around again. I looked back at the control room. Julian leaned in close to me and I wonder for a split second if he wanted to kiss me.

"Deb. It's your goddamned *cell phone*."

I managed to fish the thing out of my pocket and flip it open. I had no time to say hello before I heard Nigel from the BBC's nasal British whine. He was loud, and everyone in the room could hear him. "Deb. Brilliant. We just landed tonight in Atlanta. We're downstairs. We want to film Imena in the MRI machine."

"How did you…" I started.

"Tell him *no*," Julian said.

"No," I told Nigel.

"Deb. Darling, we're already here. We're at the back landing here. Just come let us in."

"Tell him *Hell no*," Julian said.

"*No,*" I told Nigel.

"Hang up on him," Julian said.

"We're not leaving, Deb. The world needs to see this! Now where's the MRI room, darling?"

"Hang up on him," Julian said.

I snapped the phone shut.

"Now you've got to go down there and make sure they don't get in," he said.

I nodded at him. I still didn't move.

"Go, Deb!"

I ran out the door and back down the hallway, found the big elevator and punched the starred button for the ground floor, stood holding my breath with my arms wrapped around me, staring at the dirty white wall of the elevator until it landed on the ground floor, then winged out of it to the door where we had come in and opened it. Outside were Nigel and six other people with cameras and boom mikes, standing there ready to rush the door.

"Deb, brilliant, thanks so much," Nigel said, and moved to

brush past me.

"You can't," I stuttered and blocked them with my body. "You can't film inside. I'm sorry."

Nigel grabbed the door to pull it open all the way and I snatched it back, sticking my fingernails inside the push bar, leaning back with all my weight and pulling it so they couldn't get in, my heels slipping underneath me, slowly sliding, pulling and sliding, but the door was on a delay thing and so it moved centimeters, millimeters, my arm muscles still tight and sore from lifting Imena, till the door finally slowly closed and I crashed onto the floor on my butt. At least the door was closed and they couldn't get in.

I took a deep breath and sat there on the floor for just a second. Then my cell phone rang again.

"Where are you?" Julian said. "Get back up here!"

When I got back into the room, they'd already gotten Imena into the machine and were finishing up strapping her down to the scanner bed. I helped them cover her body with more white sheets and the resident set up the IV of propofol she'd get continuously during the 30-minute scan.

"We're all still whispering like we're afraid we'll wake her up," Christine said. "But when the scan starts, that thing's going to make a banging sound like six lawnmowers."

Then the resident went into the control room in the corner and gestured through the glass for us to come in with him. We all squeezed into the tiny room. Then no one was left in the big room but Imena, masked and covered in sheets, her arms strapped to her sides.

The resident started the MRI machine. Even from the soundproof control room, it sounded like a jackhammer in an aircraft hangar. Julian rubbed his eyes behind rimless glasses, said he wished we could smoke. Imena's feet inched forward slowly, approaching the machine's barrel.

That was when Julian saw Imena's right arm. He bounced off the wall and leaned into the window, peering into the big room. Her arm was so long that part of it hung over the edge of the scanner bed, its fuzzy black fur hanging down about three inches, floating slowly toward the inside of the machine.

"Her arm!" He said, looking around wildly at us.

Christine stared out the window with her mouth open.

"It's going to slip off," she whispered. "It's going to ruin the scan."

"It's going to rip her arm off," Julian said, and before anybody can stop him he ran back out into the room.

"You can't go back in there!" the resident yelled at him, but he was already gone.

He'd forgotten that the MRI is a magnet. You can't be in the room with anything metal. And he forgot to take his glasses back off when he ran into the room.

We watched him reach down and try to stuff Imena's arm back into the strap. We saw him start flailing around and freaking out when the machine ripped his glasses off and pulled his hair out by the roots, but it was so loud in there that we couldn't hear him yelling.

8

She wants to bite me.

It was actually about a week before I noticed Marc had stopped speaking to me for real. It was just that we were so busy during the weekdays with the business of caring for Chloe, getting her to and from school and fed and changed. I know she got potty trained during that time, but I don't remember many of the details — mostly her teachers worked with her on it, spending hours taking her to and from the bathroom, sitting reading books with her about going to the potty, teaching her to learn when she had to go. By the time she got home at night we were all so tired we didn't usually mess much with it. Marc says now it nearly consumed him, all the talk of pottying, but I just don't remember. So it was the weekend before I realized something was wrong.

The night I got home from taking Imena to the hospital for her MRI, he'd made us dinner. When I didn't come home, he just took the meatloaf out of the oven, set it on the stove and left it there. I don't think he even ate any of it. Two settings were left at the table at the ready, clean wineglasses near each one. There was a basket of rolls wrapped up in a cloth napkin and a stick of butter on a side plate. There was a wilted salad. Chloe's pink and purple plastic dishes sat rinsed in the sink. I didn't notice any of it until I woke up the next morning and pulled out a chair from the table to sit and drink my coffee, looking out over all the food through the front window. Marc and Chloe had already left for work and school.

At the time I thought if Marc had been mad he would have left a note, waited up and yelled at me, something. Of course that wasn't his way. He just ate his anger, swallowed it down. When I'd pass him in the hallway at home he'd start looking like he was about to bring it back up. I'd ask him what was wrong, he'd say nothing, we'd get nowhere except further apart, and I'd float farther away.

I thought about how the lab was filling me up, puffing up my life, the apes like the inhabitants of a foreign city with a language I wanted to learn but still couldn't speak. All the most important parts of me were coming loose from the apartment, with its beige walls and nondescript furniture, decorated by Marc's cell phone sales literature and Chloe's Barbies and her pink and purple blanket, and being sucked up by the lab's centrifugal forces. By Soraya's forces, dark and scented like hyacinth, rich and loamy and adorned with long dark hair both human and ape, drum beats, charcoal prints, leaves and woods, the pull of the real earth. It was warm and gentle, and as it ripped me away from Marc, I never really felt it tear. …

Soraya's boots crunched the pine needles as she bent back tree branches so we could walk together down the path. She smelled like the Cutters Backwoods Off we'd both put all over each other to walk in the woods. Sometimes if I wore my hiking boots she'd take me out to a secret clearing in the woods behind the building to see the apes work on research tasks.

She had to know how much I loved it those few times we took walks in the woods, how after the first one I'd dashed out to Wal-Mart on my lunch hour and picked up a pair of hiking boots to keep under my desk. I would go to work each morning dressed like a normal office person, and then when I got there I'd switch out my flats for boots and shorts and lab t-shirt, well-worn ones they kept around for the caretakers to clean cages. They had lots on a shelf in a cabinet in the bathroom, and my favorite was moss green, with a watercolor-like painting of Faraji's face broken out in a happy smile.

I think we only went out together in the woods about three times during the period I worked at the lab. As we walked, she'd point out the names of trees and vines. I'd never told her I grew up in a city and didn't know their names myself. She could just tell. At the time I wanted to believe she was teaching me, quietly and a little each day, how to live in her world. I wanted to stop her and ask her what she felt for me, what it meant when we were here at night, how I was supposed to live now, what the hell I was supposed to do. But I couldn't bring it up. She had to be the one. And she never did.

Of course Marc had taught me a lot about being out in the woods, so it was easy to feel at home outside with her. He'd been into trees since he was a kid, and forestry had been a natural for him. We'd been on countless hikes where he'd shown me things like the difference between a live oak and a loblolly pine; that those big shiny bugs weren't cockroaches but scarab beetles; that the woodpeckers with the red heads like thick shag carpeting mated for life. It just wasn't until I was in the woods with Soraya that I really heard all of those things; they didn't seem to sink in until she said them. It never occurred to me that she probably didn't know anything more about the woods than Marc did.

There was a warmth in her voice I always listened for, that hint that everything she said was for me alone, the benefit of 20 years of training in science brought to bear just to impress me, to teach me. It made me breathless to think that a mind big as hers was focused on me for even a second. I wanted to go and live in the woods with her. She became the outdoors for me, she became freedom, even as she never noticed it, refused to see how I was coming apart right in front of her. Then every night I'd go home with my head full of facts, thinking about trees and sun while I changed Chloe's diapers, hemmed in by my life's beige walls, unable to breathe.

I think it was the second walk we took together, her leading me and me willing her to reach for my hand but she didn't, when we came through the thick woods to the clearing. Just before we reached it, I started to hear a faint, irregular click-click-click noise. It was Faraji, sitting cross-legged in the clearing, clicking two rocks together. Christine sat about a dozen feet away, watching, holding a long rope lead. Soraya stopped at the edge of the clearing and motioned to me.

"He's flint-knapping," she told me. "It's the same way the first humans used to make tools. He's learned just the right angle to hit the rocks against each other to make things. He loves doing it."

She sat down right there on the path and motioned for me to sit next to her.

"My friend Alex Shade brought the rocks. He's an anthropologist from the University of Albany. We've got a grant together that looks at how Faraji makes tools in the same way the ancient humans did. I think Faraji has gone through, like, six hundred pounds of rocks now," she giggled.

We watched him. We were hidden from the sunshine by thick green leaves, but it shone on him like a spotlight. I wondered if bonobos could sweat. I asked Soraya but she didn't answer, just looked across the grass at him.

Faraji focused down on the rocks, click, clicking one against the other. If he saw her he didn't show it. He just sat with the rocks in front of him, his back and massive arms rounded, and somehow funneled all that force into the pinpoint of energy he needed to break the rocks apart into smaller bits. That's why he made clicks, not thwacking or slamming.

He shifted a bit after a few minutes and cradled one bocce ball-sized rock in his hand, resting against his full, round belly, hitting it with another rock. He'd started a small pile of rock tools just to his left, and when he was through with one he'd put it on the pile and start another.

I couldn't see what was in the pile from where we sat on the grass. When Soraya said "tools" I imagined a small, shapely grey rock spoon, one Faraji would use later to eat corn kernels or beans.

"I love when Alex comes," Soraya whispered. "He brings all this rock, a truckload of it. Quartz and obsidian, mostly. None of the other apes seem to care, but for Faraji it's like Christmas. When Alex comes..." she smiled broadly and stared at Faraji. "It's like Christmas."

And that comment was like falling into a deep pit with sharp sticks poking me, ripping my skin all the way down. She'd slept with this Alex guy too. Of course.

It was the moment I realized she didn't love me. Or maybe she did, but she loved so many people, and I was simply one in a crowd, and not even a very interesting one. Thin, blonde, boring – maybe the most interesting thing about me was that I had a husband and a child. Maybe the most interesting thing about me was that I had the most to lose.

She didn't seem to care that I'd never been with a woman

before, that I'd never even really thought about it. That before her it had been only men and not even all that many. She didn't seem to care that I couldn't sleep with or even look at or talk to Marc anymore. She was not going to deal with me. She'd ripped me apart from everybody I loved, and I'd gone willingly, but now we were suspended in mid-air, just hanging, something that happened weeks ago that didn't matter much to her. I kept waiting for her to open her mouth and say something different, but she never did, and thoughts of her with other people were starting to crowd out everything else in my life. We sat there on the ground together and I kept waiting, kept waiting for her to clear her throat and look me in the eyes, change the subject to us. Instead she'd lecture to me. She did it that day in the woods.

"Leakey said that stone tools show us ancient human behavior in fossilized form. It's like a snapshot of the transition from the time the early hominids ripped their food apart with their teeth to the moment where they used tools to cut into it."

Now Faraji seemed to want to try something new and stood up, putting a new rock right where he'd been sitting. He took another in his right hand, and then he stopped and stood back, staring at them for a minute. He reached his left hand around to scratch behind his ear, just looking and thinking about it.

You have to know I felt like a spoiled stupid child, my face hot as I kept willing her to look at me like she had before. She stared at him and I stared at the back of her head. I knew I was seeing and hearing things the graduate students would kill for. If she'd taken one of them into her confidence – which for all I knew she had, but then why was I out here with her and not one of them? – it would be all they'd need, this ushering into a world of light toward a career in science. All the pieces would fall into place if she'd just take one of them by the hand, show them what she was showing me. Help them write up papers and monographs or sketch out a research trial they could do with the apes on the weekends. It was why they were here. It wasn't why I was here. I was supposed to be inside doing paperwork, trying hard to disguise the fact from everyone that I loved her.

It really was all I could do to pretend like I was listening, to ask questions that made her think I was paying attention to her work, when by now all I wanted was her. It made me angry all day every day, in a way that was becoming a part of me.

"Do apes do this kind of thing in the wild?" I finally asked her.

She looked almost embarrassed.

"Well – no. They don't. Not in the wild. They do use tools in the wild, a lot – they'll put a stick into a hole in the ground to get termites or ants. Or they'll throw a rock at a nut to crack it open.

"They don't flint-knap on their own, no. But their brains are roughly the same size as an early hominid, so if we pay attention we can tell a little about, say, how the earliest humans in stone-age Africa thought, how they moved around, how they perfected this skill. And it's fascinating that Faraji has just taken to it so well."

It was quiet in the clearing, and I guess Christine could hear us. She stopped watching Faraji then and looked over at me.

"Problem with that is once we give Faraji two tons of obsidian, we're not just observers of the research process anymore. If we feed him these neat things to do, it doesn't matter if he can do them well or not. We can't really use it for our research because we've inserted ourselves into the process."

Soraya still seemed embarrassed. She'd grabbed a handful of pine needles and was picking them apart with a fingernail.

"That's really a problem?" I asked her.

Soraya nodded.

"It's a big problem," she said. "We can't be seen as influencing him. If we do, then everything he can do, our critics will say we taught him. So they'll say there's no evidence that all or even most apes can do the things Faraji can do. People will just say he's a trained circus ape. But look at him."

He'd stood up as we talked, and we all watched him stand as tall as he could over the grey ball of obsidian on the ground, so rough and dry it was the only thing, apart from the grass and Faraji himself, that didn't brilliantly reflect the sunshine. He stared at it, preparing for the kill. Then he raised up his straight right arm almost like a discus thrower, and hurled the second rock at it with a loud thwack.

"I mean, look at him," Soraya laughed. "He loves it."

"But no, I can't write about it," she said, looking back at me. "I can't study it, or really do much beyond putting up a photo on the website. I tried that. They said it was like training a dog to fetch a ball."

"Who?" I asked her. "Who said that?" All of a sudden I was protective, ready to fight Soraya's detractors, even if the first of them was Christine.

She laughed and gazed back at Faraji.

"Well. I have many critics, of course, who say Faraji can't really use language, that he's just asking for food, or that his communication with his siblings isn't really anything important. I fight those battles every day. But on this I have to give it to them. I can't devote hours to training him and then say, 'Look, world! Look how smart Faraji is!'" Now she pointed to the black lab who followed her everywhere (though he hadn't been around that night we went out in the woods together, thank God) sitting behind us on the path. "Bob here, or some other dog might well be able to do this if he had opposable thumbs."

Ok, I thought, if I'm in the role of the student, if that's the only way to get her to talk to me, I'm game.

"But Bob couldn't make the doggie bite the snake, or put the basketball in the refrigerator, because he doesn't understand symbols like Faraji does?" I said, feeling like an undergraduate again.

She beamed at me.

"That's right. Or he might but we just don't know how to ask yet. Who knows?"

She looked back and forth between Faraji and me.

"If we took the time to make a computer where the buttons were big enough that a dog could hit them with his paw, who knows what Bob could do? But Faraji — and by extension most of the encultured apes at our lab — taught himself to do it, wanted to know what the symbols meant, waited for the opportunity to show us what he could do and then wowed us. The stone-tool making, we showed him. So we used grant money to buy the rocks, but there's not a whole lot we can do with the data."

As she said this she looked back down at the pine needles, torn up in her hands.

We both watched Faraji again, and Christine had gone silent as he sat back down and picked up a smaller rock for some detail work.

"He's awesome, though."

She stared at him like a smitten child, my stomach turned over and clenched into a cold metal ball, and I thought excellent, now I'm jealous of an ape.

It had already been a big day for my learning about bonobo culture. When I had free moments between paperwork battles and phone calls I'd surf the Internet in my office, looking for video and magazine articles about apes of all kinds. The week before I found an amazing *National Geographic* piece about Silverback mountain gorillas that kept me entertained and my actual work undone for two hours.

So far, most of what I'd found out about bonobos surrounded sex. They had it all day, every day, in every conceivable fashion and position, mothers with sons, sisters with brothers, dominant males with everyone, male or female, family or no. They form matriarchal societies, with all the slights and bitchiness you would expect in a woman-dominated posse, and they used sex for procreation, recreation and to keep the peace. If you were happy and you were a bonobo, you had sex to celebrate. If you were in an argument, you had sex to make up.

It wasn't careful study of the research that made me realize this. It was the fact that, after a week of searching the Intenet, all I'd found apart from Faraji fan sites were ones devoted to bonobo sex. The last one I'd found was so graphic I'd looked around to see if anybody was watching me, snapped my laptop shut and went to talk to Julian.

His office was just past Ardelle's reception area, and I'd begun a habit of dropping by to keep him up to date on what I'd been learning. I found an empty plastic chair behind him and just sat, realizing I didn't have a question yet.

He spun around in his chair and raised his eyebrows.

"Just…what is with all the sex?" I asked him.

Julian laughed. "They didn't tell you about that part? That's a big part of being a bonobo. You know that's why Malika and Imena are pregnant all the time."

I said it seemed like there was so much sex that it would leave precious little time for research trials.

"Yeah, that's what you'd think, but have you ever noticed we don't seem to see them actually doing it much?"

Now I was embarrassed, staring at the tile floor rather than looking right at Julian while he talked. It occurred me that I hadn't had much sex with Marc since before Chloe was born. That was probably why I had careened toward Soraya, but I couldn't see it at the time. The bonobos not only made time for sex, it was the framework for how they spent the most time. It was a way of life for them. I got so deep into thinking about it all, about Soraya, Chloe, about how churned up my stomach was all the time now, I missed most of what Julian was saying.

"Yeah, well, that's why it was confusing to me that there are about 75 bonobo sex websites," I managed.

"That's the thing. In the wild, sex is Job 1, but here they kind of keep it to themselves. They don't really broadcast it. I've been wondering if we're not passing on our own sense of sexual shame to them, you know? I've been wanting to look into it, you know, from a research standpoint, but I've got way too much on my plate right now. Here," he reached down to grab the leg of my plastic chair to pull it closer to his computer. "My colleague in San Diego sent this the other day. Check this out."

This was back when we did have Internet video, but it took forever to load, so we sat self-consciously together waiting for at least four minutes. We didn't really know each other well enough to make small talk exactly, so I looked out the window.

Then a zoo scene came up on the four-inch web screen. It was a gaggle of what looked like pink-faced first-graders in the glass-enclosed ape room. Both boys and girls had on matching plaid school shirts and floppy cotton hats, and they all spoke in crisp British accents.

The kids watched a male bonobo walk over to a female, climb on and unceremoniously get down to business. Most of the kids freaked out, turning their faces away, running to the arms of the two teachers in attendance, who could be heard laughing. Someone in the way background just muttered, "Oh my God.

Oh my God." "Eww!" yelled several of the children.

You could hear the teachers in the background; one said to the other, "I'm sorry I'm laughing," and they were both hysterical.

"At the zoo I guess they realize they have no privacy and so they do what they want. They make a show out of it. You bet that male ape knew who was watching, and that he registered the kids' reactions," Julian said. "Here it's not as much of a performance. It's almost as though they're trying to preserve the mystique, whereas a guy like this" — he nodded back toward the freeze-framed video. "I tend to wonder about a guy like that, don't you?"

I didn't really know what to say. Julian chuckled then. "That's not to say they don't do it, a lot. I've walked in on them a couple of times."

"Do they stop?" I managed.

"When I walk in? No," he laughed. "That's another reason my little project has never gotten off the ground. When I do walk in on them doing it, it's….it's not like they seem ashamed or anything. It's just what they do."

He shrugged. Then he glanced at a pile of data he was working on and back at me, and my sex lesson was over. The ape was still freeze-framed on the video, behind the glass of the zoo room, where a blonde kindergarten girl in a pink hat hid her face in her teacher's bosom.

"So now you know about bonobo sex," he said, grinning. "Welcome, Deb."

It was lucky I didn't have a ton of paperwork that day, because it was later, after lunch, that Soraya took me out to see Faraji work in the woods. I was sitting with her thinking about the video, but not knowing how to ask her about it. Then Christine seemed to signal to her that it was time for us to go back inside.

"Deb," Soraya said my name in a whisper, stood up and

reached down for my hand. "Let's go. Faraji's done and Christine can't leave until we go."

I didn't move. Suddenly I realized how strange it was going to feel to leave that scene, to just stand up walk away back down the path, as though Faraji was another human like Christine, who'd wave goodbye to us and say he'd see us later.

"We really have to keep things quiet when we come and go, Deb," Soraya said, reading my thoughts, still holding out her hand.

The BBC Film crew was still around then. Soraya had them holed up in her office, filming Malika grooming the babies and Imena lounging around asking for blueberries through the big Lexan window, the one where I'd initially met Faraji. For the first time that afternoon, I realized there weren't any cameramen out there with us, though they doubtless wanted to be. When I wasn't doing paperwork or looking at sex websites, I'd go see where they were, get their lunch orders and make sure they weren't making anybody mad. But Soraya had just guided them to where she wanted them to think the action was (usually just the graduate students doing trials and feeding) and the BBC guys never seemed to notice that Soraya, herself, wasn't around much. They'd come from Europe to film her and the apes and every day, they were missing all the good stuff. Despite everything I was feeling then, I did feel lucky that she'd occasionally just walk out to the woods, with me, me and Faraji, where everything was really happening.

As she pulled me up to standing, she said, "Between the Malika and Imena and the babies and the film crew, Faraji just can't think when he's in there," nodding toward the Main Building.

I stood up, but every part of me wanted to keep sitting there on the path with her. I thought if I could just keep sitting there, in the warm sun with the smell of the pine trees and her hair,

I couldn't help but figure everything out. Even her pulling me toward her, then rushing away. Even the hours I was spending every week slinking through just looking for her and never finding her. Even when I gave up at the end of the day and just went up to her closed, quiet office door and touched it once really quickly so that nobody saw. Even that.

That's my memory of that day, of quiet, of Faraji in the woods, working as if we weren't there, barely registering us as the sun hit his skin, gripping the stones with long, brittle nails in black padded hands. I'd start to think of Faraji the famous ape as just another human lab staff member until I really stared at those hands that day in the woods. They were less like an animal's and more like those of a man from another planet. A man from another planet who needed quiet time in the woods to make things, whose mother and sister drove him crazy while their babies jumped up and down and onto his shoulders to play all the time, who was a little keyed up lately because he didn't have a girlfriend. A man who Soraya would really rather not be around a six-man BBC film crew, not because they'd disrupt the research process, but because he'd feel like he was in competition with those men for every woman in the room, whether human or ape.

The next morning I decided to go in a little late and pack a lunch for Chloe to take to preschool. I was stuffing baby carrots in a sandwich bag in with a peanut butter sandwich I'd already set neatly in her backback. Then Marc made his way to the front door with Chloe in his arms. He picked the carrots out of my hand and set them down on the counter. I asked him what the hell he was doing.

"The school makes Chloe's lunch now. She eats a school lunch," he said crisply, turning his back to me, moving to pick up his keys.

I stared gape-mouthed at the back of his head.

"Since when?" I managed.

They turned back to face me, Chloe looking lazily at me over a purple sippy cup, Marc staring.

"About a month ago. Pay attention," he said evenly, then they were out the front door and gone.

I pulled in to the parking lot and Julian was behind me in his green Jetta. I got out slowly, balancing a travel mug of coffee and my bag, but Julian screeched into his space and wriggled his paperthin body out of his car and ran past me with his cell phone pressed to his ear. In the moment he passed, I could hear Christine talking quickly on the other end. He swung open the front door and went inside.

Everything was quiet for the first minute I was inside. Ardelle's computer was on, but she wasn't at her desk. Julian had run past his own office and straight to the back to Soraya's. Nobody else was in the front of the building, but Ardelle's radio was in her chair. It crackled and came to life.

"Soraya, this is Julian. Where is Clara?" came Julian's voice.

A beat, then, urgent and angry, again, "Where is Clara? Where is Kalala?"

When Soraya came on, she sounded calm.

"This is Soraya. Clara is with me. We're in the back. She's safe now."

"Did you call 911?" came Julian's voice. "Did anybody call 911?"

No answer. I went to Julian's office first, looking for any of the graduate students he shared the space with. No one was there.

"Julian, this is Soraya. Come to the back. Uba is pulling the Tahoe around. He'll take Clara to the hospital."

I knocked on the doors of the other five offices in the Main building. No one answered.

When I got back to the front, Ardelle was sitting at her desk. She held up both hands as I raced toward her.

"She's okay. She's okay," she said. "It's just her fingers. Faraji bit her fingers. On her right hand. Just her fingers."

Ardelle's eyes were bugging out. I'd run up to the desk and now was close enough to touch her, and I think I just stood over her, staring with my mouth open.

"It's bad, Ms. Deb," she said, staring at me. "It's really bad."

I kept staring at her. She didn't mean Faraji attacking Kalala; she meant this whole place. She meant every square foot of the lab. All the land it was on, every foot up to her chair and her desk. She sat on her rolling secretary's chair like she was afraid to put her weight on it. She held her hands out at the elbows, afraid to touch anything.

I made myself breathe, sat down slowly, afraid to make any sudden movements or Ardelle would go off like a bomb.

"How did he get to her?" I finally asked her.

"Clara was putting food in his box, and he beckoned her over to the corner of the cage where he was playing with something," she said. It was a knife. She told him to put it down, and then he came to the fence and grabbed her hand through the chain link.

"He seemed," she lowered her voice, pulling her chin down, rounding her shoulders into a shaking ball. "Uba said he seemed upset with her. I know that's crazy, but that's what Uba said."

"So he bit her….to make a point?" I asked. "That's asinine."

Ardelle shrugged, the tops of her shoulders coming up almost to her ears, then back down. I thought she looked just like a little bird.

"Or he bit her because he's an ape, and that's what they do," she sighed now and looked up at me. "I don't know what to think, Deb."

"Where did Faraji get a knife?" I was pacing back and forth now in what little room was left in the reception area. "Why did they give him a knife?"

"I don't think anybody gave it to him," Ardelle said, reaching behind her to pick up the bowl of stone tools Faraji had with him the woods the day before. She held it between us. "When no one was looking, he must have hidden one of these."

She palmed one of the flakes from the bowl from yesterday. I should have realized, of course, when Soraya had told me early humans had used these same tools to rip into flesh for food, but I'd still envisioned...I don't know, arrowheads, maybe crude spoons. These were razor-sharp knives. Faraji had made a bowl full of weapons.

...

Kalala was in the hospital, Marc was absolutely not speaking to me, and the photographer from the *London Times* was scheduled to come in that day. I remembered as I skulked back to my office, holding my stomach. I was starting to dread any press coming anywhere near the lab. They'd promised they could just shoot the apes through the windows or the chain link, but I knew that, inevitably, they'd start whining about how they weren't getting any good film. They'd casually mention, 67 times a day, how much they'd like to go inside the enclosures or take the apes out so they could get some really good photos.

This was, of course, one hundred percent out of the question. I'd already had several calls from downtown, panicked calls from Ben Hooper, the assistant VP everybody called Eeyore, calls that would start out all, "How are you making out? Good!"

and progress quickly to "You have to promise me that no one outside of Soraya and Julian and Christine ever goes into those enclosures, Deb. That especially means the press. We cannot have people getting bitten."

I asked Christine once what she thought would happen if the blonde-haired black woman reporter from WATA were to get bitten, or the Nova reporters who did a big story on Faraji years ago, or even one of these BBC cameramen who seemed always to be underfoot these days. She looked at me for a second, as if she was surprised I was so stupid.

"Well," she'd looked around and then waved her hand a bit, at the buildings, the trees, the road leading in from civilization to our own ape haven. "All of this would just go away. We'd lose everything."

I'd worked in universities for years by then, and I made some joke about how everything takes months or years to happen on college campuses. You have to convene committees that meet several times over the course of a semester, and write memos and proposals and make phone calls and get into arguments. Nothing happens without seemingly endless preps and posturing and everything takes at least a year. Christine listened patiently and smiled a little and looked down at her sneakers.

"No," she said, shaking her head. "No, I think if they wanted to shut us down it would probably go pretty fast."

The thought stopped me cold. The lab was more my home now than my real home. I was my real self there, and only there. If the lab closed, I would…what would I do exactly? Go home and back to Marc? Take care of Chloe fulltime? I couldn't see my way out of the muck of Soraya.

I actually knew the photographer who was coming today. He was Stewart Linn, the one who'd taken that first photo of Joie the baby ape and splashed it on the front page of the Sunday edition of the *London Times*. He'd called a couple of weeks back and asked to be allowed a return visit for an in-depth feature on Soraya's different projects. Soraya remembered Stewart, said he was nice, and sure, he could come back for a visit. But only for a few days, and I was to help keep him back away from the fences and a good ways from any actual action.

By this time Imena's pregnancy made her so ornery that even her favorite staff members were starting to have trouble dealing with her.

"For awhile, it was nothing you couldn't fix by just calling a halt to whatever you were trying do to go and get her some Taco Bell," Christine said. I'd pulled her into my office to try to work out some last-minute logistics on Stewart's visit. "But lately that kind of thing is happening more often. She won't cooperate unless you go get her something, whether it's blueberries or burritos or M&Ms or a movie, and then you go and get it for her, and then she won't cooperate at all. She's just a bitch."

"Do you think she'll cooperate for Stewart? Soraya said she worked well with Stewart the last time," I said, the sound of her name on my lips both thrilling me and making me feel sick. I was leaning against my desk, and I felt for a second like my knees might buckle and I might fall to the floor.

I knew Soraya was working on a paper designed to show that bonobos possessed a wide range of cultural abilities like painting and music, but apparently Imena had stopped playing along weeks before.

"Sure, she likes Stewart. She likes me, too. She's not gonna do a goddamned thing for Stewart, I'll be you a hundred bucks," Christine sighed and held up her half-bitten hand. "I only got a few fingers left on this one," she said, staring into her hand. "I'd like to keep them."

Then she heaved herself out of my chair, muttered about having to go get things ready, and left.

Stewart was due to stay a whole week, but he started getting antsy right away. He was so sweet, just an unkempt boy really, with unruly brown hair and those teeth Londoners are famous for, who wore wrinkled button-down Oxfords and jeans. He didn't make me go out and get him lunch and he sat and ate McDonald's in the break room with us without complaining. We were already starting to treat him like one of the staff.

But he came to see me late in the afternoon of the first day and sat down in my office in the extra chair, and then he put his head in his hands.

"It's…I'm sorry. I know, I promised to shoot them through the chain link. I know. But I'm not getting anything. And I'm sending the people back in London thumbnails of what I am getting. Which is not much at all. And they're getting really nervous."

I thought back to the photo Stewart had taken of Joie. Christine had been holding him like a toddler, him facing her with his legs wrapped around her waist, looking back over her shoulder. You saw Joie's amazing face snuggling up under Christine's ponytail. It was the first photo I'd ever seen from the lab and it had made me want to know more about it. I told Stewart that.

"Yes, that's the problem, dear, see…" he got up and closed my office door, then came back and sat down next to me. "Christine won't do that anymore, she says Joie's getting too big now. Too heavy for her to carry, and big enough so that if he decided he wanted to bite me, well, he could.

"Soraya won't let me near Faraji because he's jealous of me, so that leaves Imena. I know they take her out in the woods for walks every day, but they won't let me near when they do. I signed every liability form they've thrown at me, and sorry, dear, you've thrown at me. Look, I am not going to sue. She's not going to bite me. I've just got to get some pictures. Can you help me get some pictures? Can you ask Soraya to let me go out with them today?"

So I did.

When I walked back to her office, she was hunched over her laptop, actually scowling at it. She held nothing back, never thought to put on a brave face, just showed you what was going through her mind at any moment by the look in her eyes. She was like Chloe in that way, so present. When she looked at you she was really looking at you, not thinking of something else she had to do. This semester she had four graduate students, three different funded grant projects and who knew how many papers for different journals. But she brought that presence to every encounter. Except when I'd really needed to talk to her. Then she was just gone.

Now I was breaking her concentration and forcing her to look up at me. I couldn't tell if she saw a friend or a lover or a subordinate, and she didn't give me any clues. I laid it all out for her, apologizing again and again, feeling guilty for suggesting Stewart come back in the first place, for every interruption of her work that my work stood for. She just looked at me, and there was no anger, just tiredness, which made me feel worse, but beg harder. About halfway though I started to think: just this once, just do this quickly and it'll be over, let's just get this over.

In the end she nodded, said "okay," and went back to scowling at her laptop, and I left feeling like a silly, dancing court jester. But I held up my head about halfway back to my office, then walked in to tell Stewart okay, he could come out in the woods with us that afternoon.

The outing felt weird from the start. Christine didn't say anything but was kind of tight-lipped in general the whole afternoon. I couldn't tell if she was upset about Stewart or something else, but I never had a chance to pull her aside and talk to her about it.

That was the day I really got to know Imena. She was so pregnant she had pretty much stopped walking very far at all anymore. I'd watched her in the enclosure though, and marveled that when she did want to move — to go over and scold one of the baby apes if they were all in there together, or to get something she wanted — she could still move fast. As she led us out into the sunlight, Christine chuckled about having to barter with Imena to go outside every morning so they could clean her enclosure.

"Her other babies are over in Building C, and you'd think she wants to go see them, but no," Christine smiled and watched the ground as she gripped Imena's lead. Then she stopped, turned back to face Stewart and I, and held her hand up.

"Listen, okay, I'm going to need you two to hang back a bit," she said. "You've got to keep about a dozen feet between you and Imena. For safety."

Stewart was fiddling with some equipment hanging in a black canvas bag from his chest and not looking at her. So she waited until he met her eyes and nodded, and then Stewart and I followed slowly.

I started using my arms to guide Stewart like I did when I was out with Chloe in parking lots, sort of guiding her body with my hands but not actually touching her, making a kind of safety force field around us. I held both arms straight down but fanned them out to show her where to be, to slow her down when she went too fast. It annoyed her and sometimes she'd swat back at my hands. I didn't realize I was doing it with Stewart until we'd gone about thirty feet from the lab's back door to the path that led through the woods, and once I did see what I was doing I felt embarrassed but couldn't really stop myself.

Stewart didn't seem to mind. I think he realized that was the cost of being outside with Imena. He knew Soraya didn't have to let him anywhere near her.

Imena loped out into the daylight with a collar around her neck. We started out from the main building with Christine carrying her lead and a paper version of the keyboard the apes used to communicate.

"Where do you want to go today, Imena? Should we go see the babies in Building C, do you think?" Christine asked brightly.

Imena stopped in her tracks and pointed at the plastic keyboard. Christine bent down to see what she was pointing to.

"You want to go see Soraya? Let me call her on the radio. I'm not sure where she is…" Christine took the radio clipped to her belt and called for Soraya.

We'd come outside though the hallway that led past Soraya's office. She hadn't been inside and her door was closed. We all stopped and waited while Christine called her. Imena then leveled her gaze at Stuart and I. But it wasn't the same friendly face she'd shown to visitors who brought her blueberries. I couldn't have told you exactly how her expression was different, being so black and so far away. It was bright and her big, dusty body seemed to suck up the sun, and it was starting to twitch in a way you see men do before they draw back fists in a fight. Her eyes were flat and cold.

"Sorry —" Stewart whispered. I could tell by the way he tensed up that he'd noticed Imena too. He faltered for a second, glancing over at her, then: "Is there a key for Soraya on there? I guess I didn't realize that."

I nodded. Christine didn't seem to take note of the way Imena was looking at us. She walked over to Stewart, showing him the Soraya key, a blue silhouette of head and shoulders with no face and flowing brown hair.

"Imena's asking for Soraya. Soraya's the most important ape

102

here. The apes are always pointing at her name on the keyboard. They're always wanting to know where she is."

Soraya didn't answer Christine's call on the radio.

"Huh. Maybe she had an appointment, Imena," Christine said, walking back to where Imena stood, about fifteen feet in front of Stewart and I. She handed the keyboard back to the ape. "I don't think she's around."

Imena glared hard at Christine and pointed to the Soraya key again. Stewart lifted his camera up to his face, quickly and quietly snapping a few shots.

"Okay, hold up, Imena, let me call her again," Christine said. "Julian, this is Christine," she called into the radio. "Any idea where Soraya is right now?"

We all of us listened for a minute to the static and silence of the radio.

"Nope," Julian responded.

"Ape lab, this is Christine. Anybody know where Soraya is right now?"

Imena stood stock still and stared at Christine while she made the radio calls. She reminded me of a harried mother at the checkout counter at a grocery store, when the checkout girl kept having to do price checks, about to lose her temper and start yelling. When she turned to look at us, I wasn't close enough to really see, but it felt like a blank, hostile stare.

Christine's radio finally crackled to life.

"This is Uba Youlou," came the big man's baritone. "What is the problem?"

"Uba, we've got Imena out behind the main building on a lead, and she's asking for Soraya. Any idea where she is?"

It seemed to take Uba a long time to respond, then:

"Ms. Soraya is not available now."

"Ah," said Christine. "Not available. Imena, Soraya's not available right now." I think she wanted to say something under her breath then, like I would, something like "well that's just fucking great," but Christine wouldn't dare. She just turned her radio off and clipped it back to her belt.

"Well, where else would you like to go, Imena? How about we go see Joie in Building C?" She pointed to the key for Joie and held it up so Imena could see.

Imena glared at Christine then and held out her arm for the keyboard. In that moment I think Christine started to feel Imena's anger too. She handed the keyboard to Imena, and Imena pointed to Soraya again.

"Well, let's just go for a walk, then, Imena, and we'll see where we end up." Then Christine started forward, lightly pulling the lead. Imena stood right where she was for a second, and then moved forward grudgingly.

I didn't realize I'd been holding my breath until it came out in a gust. We walked without talking through the leaves for about 50 feet, to a clearing behind the main building near a chain link tunnel that the apes used to move between the buildings. Faraji sat in the tunnel, scratching his underarm and watching us.

"Look, Imena, it's Faraji!" Christine said brightly. "Hi, Faraji!"

Faraji pant-hooted and scratched his underarm again.

"Faraji, say hi!" Christine called.

Faraji let loose with gradually louder hoots, starting off as low grunts we could talk over and escalating into a screaming "oohwah! Oowah! OOWAH!" that hurt the inside of your ears. Imena ignored him. She walked up to the chain link and stopped about ten feet away. She sat down in the grass. Christine brought her the keyboard and dropped it on the ground next to her, then knelt a few feet away.

Imena pointed at Stewart and me. Christine followed her eyes and said, "That's Stewart, the photographer. He's going to take your picture for the newspaper."

Imena pointed at Stewart again. Without thinking I stood closer to him and protected him with my arm. My fear spread cold from my chest and crawled up my neck.

"I know you want him to come over and say hi, but he can't, Imena. He has to stay back."

Imena looked hard at Stewart then, and then back at Christine. Then she started hooting, so loud that by the time she was done there was nothing between my ears but pain.

"Sorry, Imena, Stewart can't come over," Christine said again. She seemed wary now, like she was getting a little nervous about Imena's mood. "Let's go see the babies in Building C, Imena."

Imena pulled the plastic keyboard up onto her bulging lap. She pointed at the Soraya key again.

"Sorry, Imena, no Soraya." I remember thinking then that Christine was starting to look tired. Then I saw Imena was beckoning to her. She scooted a little closer. Imena turned so we couldn't see what she was pointing at on the keyboard, unnecessary since we were back almost 30 feet from her now, and made what sounded like a grunt in Christine's ear. Then she turned and glared at us. Christine jumped back and stood about six feet back from Imena and looked at me and started mouthing something. I couldn't make out what it was, or why she wouldn't just say it. I leaned forward but I couldn't hear what she was trying to say and I couldn't read her lips.

"Oh. It's me," Stewart hissed. "It's me. She wants to bite me."

I stared back at Christine, whose eyes were as big as saucers. She nodded very slowly and held her arm up and out at us, mouthing the words "GO. SLOWLY."

When I opened my mouth to answer her — and I still don't know what I meant to say — my cell phone rang. I flipped it open and put it to my ear. Stewart looked at me, frozen, wide-eyed. Christine stood staring at Imena.

"Ms. Solomon? Are you there? This is Ms. Lily from Sawyer Child Development Center."

I didn't answer. We all stood there looking at each other.

"Ms. Lily, from Chloe's school? Ms. Solomon, are you there?"

"Yes. I'm here. What's wrong with Lily?" I shook my head then, in two worlds at once, both of them blowing up. "I mean, sorry, what's wrong with Chloe?"

"Well, we were out on the playground and it looks like she's gotten bitten by something. A mosquito, maybe."

A mosquito. So she got bitten a mosquito. Stewart and I seemed about to get mauled by an ape. But suddenly I thought of her soft, fleshy baby skin turning red, and her crying.

"Is she okay? Is she upset?"

"Well….we can't tell. Her arm, where she got bit, is hot and swelling up. We're wondering if she's having an allergic reaction, if it might have been a bee. She's really upset. She's calling for you."

They found Chloe wherever she was in the room and put the phone up to her face, and she was screaming.

I just stood there staring at Stewart, him afraid to take his eyes off Imena, my mouth hanging open, Chloe crying.

"Mrs. Solomon, if she's having an allergic reaction to a bug bite, you'd really better take her to a doctor."

"When?" I managed.

"When?" Ms. Lily coughed. "Well, soon. Now, if possible."

"Okay." I snapped my phone shut and stood looking at Stewart and Christine. Imena shifted her weight as though she was thinking about getting up. She stared at Stewart and bared her teeth. She growled slow and low, almost under her breath. "Fuck," Stewart whispered under his breath. "GO," mouthed Christine.

I grabbed Stewart's hand then, my first thought that we'd back away slowly out of the clearing. But he whispered "Fuck!" under his breath again and in the end we just wheeled around, our boots slipping on patches of wet leaves, and ran.

9

I started thinking of him as a roommate.

It took me 20 minutes to flee the lab and speed down the interstate to Chloe's school. Maybe this is it, I thought, gripping the steering wheel and forcing people out of the left lane. Since she was born I'd felt like she was a Christmas present too precious to take out of the box, and now I'd left her out too long and she got broken. She was almost two. I wondered what had taken so long. At the time I thought if she was actually in my care during the weekdays instead of with Ms. Lily at the preschool, she wouldn't have made it past her first birthday.

I parked illegally and ran into her classroom. She was fine. She was sitting alone with her back to the door, playing with a cloth book, looking out the window at the other kids on the playground. She has thin blonde hair like mine, the afternoon sun glinting off it. Her left arm was twice its usual size, but Ms. Lily said she'd stopped minding it so much during the last few minutes. I studied her face for tracks of tears, but they were gone. Ms. Lily would have wiped them quickly away.

Chloe held out her swollen arm for me to inspect while Ms. Lily calmed me, saying sometimes kids will have a reaction to their first mosquito bite, it's not a big deal, but why don't you take her over to her doctor to get some Benadryl and have him check it out. It was like she was Chloe's real mother and mine at the same time, knowing I needed her to tell me what to do. I knew other parents of children in Chloe's class who argued with Ms. Lily, who thought she was old-fashioned and strict, but I did whatever she told me to.

I don't remember much about the doctor's visit itself. I pretended I knew what I was doing at the doctor's, like I wasn't still afraid I'd drop Chloe or accidentally poison her. Even back way before Soraya, back before Chloe could walk or talk, I kept how I felt from Marc, hiding how at sea I was with my own baby, how afraid of her I was. I didn't think he could tell, but now I know he could. Everyone could. Everyone but me.

In fact, I don't remember much about being with either Marc or Chloe during that Soraya time. I've always had such a hard time waking up in the morning, and it was easy to fall into the habit of getting up almost too late, running through a shower and coffee before packing Chloe into the car, dropping her off at school and heading to the lab. I was at my desk before I was fully awake most days. There was never enough time during the work days to walk in the woods, sit with Soraya and talk to the apes, tool around with Christine in the Tahoe or go ask Julian some question and still get all my paperwork done, so I was invariably at the lab late. Often I'd be getting home as Marc was feeding Chloe and putting her to bed.

I was standing in our kitchen telling Marc what little I knew about the bug bite that night, but he couldn't hear what I was saying. He kept turning his back to me, fiddling with Chloe's bag. Occasionally he nodded, but he wouldn't discuss it for the whole first hour we were home. Later that night, after I was starting to calm down about the bug bite and the doctor visit and the possible mauling, that's when Marc felt like talking.

"I didn't realize Ms. Lily had your phone number," he said at first.

I just shrugged. "We put both our numbers on all those forms…."

And he interrupted. "Yes, but she usually calls me."

I looked blankly at him. "Why?" I needed to be quiet, to be alone with everything, to keep trying to work it all out. Soraya… Imena…Stewart. Where had Stewart gone when I left? I'd grabbed my bag and ran to my car. He didn't have keys to get back into the building. He didn't have anywhere to hide. Here was Marc speaking up after weeks of silence, and all wanted was for him to stop talking.

"Why?" Marc said it in a whisper, icy. "Why does she always call me? Because I'm the one who always shows up."

"Oh for Christ's sake, Marc," I spat at him. Now I was never going to get any time to think. He was never going to stop talking.

"She has both our numbers." I said, exhausted, shrugging again, as though that was the whole issue. As though the numbers had anything to do with anything. I pretended not to hear him, like always, and he dropped it, like always.

Of course by then I'd started to see him as a roommate. It was as if my husband had gone away on a long trip, leaving a tall blonde, silent impostor who was so focused on keeping Chloe's bottles clean he didn't have much time to talk to me. Every time I encountered him he was doing for her, making it too easy for me to wait to bring up anything important.

Of course I knew how messed up it was that *I'd* been the one rushing across town, needed desperately while he stood in a cell phone kiosk in the mall. Of course I hadn't thought to call and tell him what was going on. Of course now that I was supposed to stand in the kitchen and explain how it had all happened, I couldn't quite put the words together, wanted only to go sit on the porch and stare down at the traffic and think about Soraya.

Then the phone rang, and it was her. She hadn't ever called me at home before. I walked to the phone in the bedroom, wondering if she'd heard about Chloe's bite and wanted to check on her. As I turned right into our hallway I thought, it's not Chloe — someone must have told Soraya about how close Imena came to attacking Stewart today. Me — Stewart and me. I was there too. Now she was calling me at home, furious, she must be furious.

I took a huge deep breath as I picked up the bedroom extension. Imena would have mauled me too. Bitten my fingers off. Or maybe they bite fingers because that's the only thing they can reach through the chain link. Outside, maybe she would have just jumped me. Maybe tried to pull my arms off. It would be easy for her. Wouldn't it?

Or what if Soraya wanted to talk about...us? But she didn't want to talk about any of those things. She didn't mention them at all.

"Listen, I am so sorry to just be telling you this now," she said breathlessly. It sounded like she was still at the lab.

"Where are you?" I asked her. "It sounds like a lot of people speaking in Japanese behind you."

"It is a lot of people speaking in Japanese," Soraya said. "There are a lot of people here right now. They're from a television station in Osaka. I forgot to tell you about the Japanese television special, didn't I?" She giggled now.

I told her I would be in early the next morning to help deal with them, and she gave a little breathless laugh.

"Well…that's the problem. They're filming tonight. They're doing a satellite linkup thing at 9:30 tonight — the show airs live in Japan, it'll be morning there."

Marc had come into the bedroom holding Chloe in one arm, some jackets on hangers to go in the closet in the other. As I said, "Tonight?" I watched him, waiting for him to shoot me an evil look, to point at her as if to ask who was going to feed her, change her, read to her, put her to bed.

But he didn't react. He just turned around with her curled up into his neck, her little arms around him, her eyes closed. You couldn't tell where his honeycolored hair stopped and hers began. They looked shiny, porcelain, together. The two of them just left the bedroom and he closed the door behind them. I'd been dismissed.

When Soraya hung up I called Christine's cell phone.

"Oh God, yes, the Japanese are here," she said, sounding tense and tired, still at the lab.

"At least it seems a little quieter where you are," I told her.

"I locked myself in your office and put a towel under the door. I really thought somebody had told you about this," she said. "Soraya apparently set all this up back in the spring. In her characteristic Soraya way of telling people they can come do stuff with the apes and not telling any of us anything about it."

"Soraya says they're filming tonight. She wants me to come back down there tonight."

"Well, yes. That would be nice," Christine said wearily. "There are a dozen Japanese schoolchildren here. They're going to go in the back with Faraji in a little while, and it would be great if we had some way of keeping them away from the windows. That's what Clara would do, and she's not here."

Christine said she too was surprised when an NHK Television

satellite truck and two vans pulled up in the parking lot a little after 6 that night. She said she'd known they were going to come eventually, sometime this fall.

"I'll tell you one thing, when you come tonight you won't be able to park in the parking lot, and make sure you stay away from their million-dollar satellite trucks or they'll curse you in Japanese."

"I thought Asians were so reserved," I chuckled at her, but she didn't laugh.

"Just when are you coming?" she said.

When I got there Julian was scuttling through the conference room carrying two bright yellow industrial-type extension cords. He looked more like a construction worker than a scientist and he was in a horrible mood. I still couldn't believe the lab had been beset by a Japanese TV crew, even though I'd walked right past a huge satellite truck with a receiver pole reaching fifty feet up into the air.

I told Julian hello quickly, and asked him if he knew which show they were here filming, at least.

"It's...it's called Super Happy Fun Show or something. I don't know what the hell it's called." Then he was gone in the back, and I followed.

Soraya's office had been turned into a makeshift TV studio. A huge monitor set up in front of her desk showed empty bleachers and microphones in a corresponding studio in Japan — the words "Osaka Broadcasting Center" ran underneath the picture. Two cameramen in jeans and hoodies duct-taped wires to the ground. It was now very quiet, and Soraya herself wasn't around.

I looked through the window leading to the ape room, which at the moment was free of apes. Inside were another two men rigging lights and sound equipment. I couldn't see anything for me to do, and I turned around to leave. Then I saw the dozen completely silent eight-year-old Japanese schoolchildren wearing identical navy Izod-type shirts with **Tennoji-ku Elementary School** stitched over the left breast. They were sitting cross-legged on the floor in two neat rows against the far wall of Soraya's office.

At the end of one of the rows sat a young Japanese woman I thought might be their keeper. She smiled broadly at me as I took them all in. She was about twenty, dressed like the riggers. She stood up immediately and came over to me. But she didn't say anything to me, just smiled.

I had no idea what I was supposed to do with the children.

"Do any of them...need anything?" I asked her.

She shook her head and smiled. "No."

"Like some water maybe?" I tried. "Maybe they'd be more comfortable in the conference room?"

She shook her head again.

"No. Thank you. They don't need."

"Well, okay," I said, willing myself to take control of what might be about to happen. "I guess when we start filming, the children will need to stay back from the window to the ape room a few feet. For safety."

She nodded and smiled at me.

"And there are parts of the wall here where there's chain link. None of the children will be allowed to get near the chain link for safety."

She nodded again before I finished the sentence, and then when I was done, she said: "We know. It's okay. They stay back. We know."

I stood there staring at all of them for a second until Julian finished delivering the extension cords and came back through the room. He knelt down and put a hand on my back.

"Here's what's going to happen, Deb. They'll go live in a few minutes and then all the TV people will be in here, Faraji will be in there. Soraya will be in with him. It shouldn't take very long. This is Yoshi," he said, nodding toward the young woman with the children. She nodded and smiled at me. Julian left the room again.

I had no idea what to do with myself, so I went and sat in my office for the next half hour, looking out my window at the rest of the riggers smoking and leaning against the satellite truck.

At 9:20 a young Japanese man with bleached blonde hair in a shiny suit climbed out from the truck. A woman about Yoshi's age in a short red gingham dress with cotton petticoats stepped out after him, gingerly stepping feet in shiny, ruby-slipper pumps over the cords duct taped to the ground. I watched them walk into the building and go straight to the back, toward the loud Japanese pop music that was now thumping out of Soraya's office. Once they were in I followed, but kept far enough back that they didn't see me until they reached the monitor and turned back around to take their places on x's masking-taped to the floor.

The Osaka studio on the monitor was now full of children on bleachers, waiting patiently while the music washed over and through them and into Soraya's office. Credits in Japanese popped on and off the screen, and the couple I'd watched walk in waved to their counterparts in Osaka, who looked older and more conservatively dressed. There were so many people on the monitor and in the room that I didn't see where there would be any room for Faraji and Soraya to fit on screen.

Yoshi stood up and pushed the children into the far corner of the office, where they stood close together on wooden risers. None of them said a single word, though some of them poked each other and giggled just a little, almost silently. They peered through the window as they passed it to catch a glimpse of Faraji, who wasn't in place yet.

The man and woman from the trucks took their place in front of the children, standing slightly off to the side. They tested their mics while the riggers crouched low at monitors and fiddled with dials near where the children had been sitting. I didn't know how they could hear themselves over the music, or how it was affecting Faraji, who I thought must be waiting to come out and be on TV. It was very loud, and the show hadn't even started. There was no sign of Soraya anywhere.

Then all of a sudden everything started. The announcer looked brightly into the camera and introduced himself and his strangely dressed young sidekick to the audience in Japanese. The kids in Atlanta waved to the kids in Osaka in their identical school shirts over the booming, bouncing happy music.

I couldn't make out a word they were saying. I went over to the spot on the floor where the kids had been and sat down cross-legged next to Yoshi to watch the monitor. She grinned beautifully at me. Julian ran back through the room after helping the riggers with some last-minute adjustment, and sat down on the floor with us. He and Yoshi started whispering.

They could see it annoyed me not to know what was going on, so Yoshi started providing commentary while still photos of Faraji flashed up on the monitor.

"They're introducing him now. They're talking about him. These students —" she pointed to the eight year-olds lined up on the risers, "have been studying Faraji for weeks now, reading books about him and other bonobos. They're like…uh —"

"They're like ambassadors," Julian said.

"Right, ambassadors for their school in Osaka. Their classmates are waiting in the studio for them to introduce Faraji and then they're all going to talk to him."

The music went down a little lower then and the picture on the monitor focused on the door to the inner enclosure, which opened on cue. Faraji ambled through, already smiling. He was by himself. He should've been in bed hours ago, but he liked this TV show thing. He was into it.

"The Japanese are in love with Faraji. Children and adults alike," Julian whispered, and Yoshi nodded.

Faraji came up to the edge of the chain link and sat down, the camera trained on his face. The kids in Atlanta and Osaka both went crazy, cooing and laughing, smiling ear to ear, all of them thrilled. You'd never see American kids react this way to Faraji. Lots of American kids who visited acted bored around him, like they'd been brought up sitting outside the ape window at the zoo. Once most kids got past the age of three or four they acted like they'd already seen the show.

Then they did the standard thing where they asked Faraji questions and he responded on the keyboard. The music never stopped and it was still hard to tell what was going on from moment to moment. It was late, I was tired, and there was so much color and movement and noise that I tuned out and stared at the floor for a minute just to let my mind calm down. Eventually, though, I thought of Ben Hooper, and it occurred to me lean in to ask who paid for all this.

Yoshi wrinkled her nose. "For all what?"

"All the TV stuff," I said dully. "The money it takes to get all of you over from Japan and beam this back to the studio in Osaka." The university was talking about possible layoffs in the spring and watching asinine things like overtime pay and paper consumption. If we'd wanted to make our videos at the lab for our students or visitors, the accountants downtown would ask us what account it was going to come out of. Julian had warned me that come January, the Arts & Sciences dean would start trolling around in the lab's accounts, looking for pots of money with nice high balances. Money we'd been saving because we knew we had to have enough in place to pay for food for the apes through June. Watch, he'll just take it and give it to other programs that have already spent all their money, Julian told me. He did it every year.

Yoshi smiled. "The network pays. The network pays for everything."

Julian looked at me.

"The network pays for this —" he pointed at the cameras and the children. One of them was enunciating in slow Japanese directly in the mic and Faraji was nodding vigorously. "And this," he said, circling his finger around his head. "Everything."

I just frowned at him.

"What do you mean?"

Julian leaned closer and whispered.

"Soraya sold the rights to film Fajaji to them about ten years ago. The network comes whenever they want. They send her like $25,000 a year. It might be more."

I didn't know about the money, and I was keeping all the accounts. I just stared at him.

"She doesn't tell anybody about it," Julian said.

"But what...?" I looked away and stared at the children. What did she do with the money? "Where is she anyway?" I asked him.

He shook his head, said he didn't know. Yoshi leaned in and whispered in my ear.

"We were up very late last night," she giggled. "She and Uba made us a wonderful dinner. And we brought some vodka so...." She leaned away again.

Uba. She was with Uba last night. And nobody knew where she was now. I was in so much trouble. I couldn't catch my breath. My stomach roiling, I stared at the floor.

Yoshi leaned back in.

"Not the children though!" she whispered. "The children went to bed."

Faraji peeled a banana and smiled at the kids in their blue shirts. He looked around to see where all the music and voices and lights were coming from, but it was all coming from everywhere.

10

This is why we're talking about dogs.

The days were getting drier. When I got to the lab the most mornings, I was so tired from the night before I felt like I was sleepwalking, my eyelids papery and heavy. I pushed open the door one morning, a few days after the Japanese episode, to see Soraya sitting inside my office. In the four seconds it took to push open the door and see her, possible reasons for her to be there went fleeting through my mind like sugar-high kids through a playground. I'd just dropped Chloe off and she'd gone tearing off like that after a friend in her hot pink sweater, disappearing into an igloo-shaped play apparatus painted primary colors, before I had a chance for a kiss goodbye. When I opened the door and saw Soraya sitting there, facing the door with a smile like a puppy, I saw all those colors again in quick, garish swooshes behind my eyes.

"Deb!" she popped up out of my chair and floated toward

the door.

"Where were you?" I grumbled at her, looking around for a place to set my purse down. Her backpack sat where I usually kept it, in the extra chair closest to the door. I spilled a little of my takeout coffee and my sandwich in a ziplock bag slipped from between my fingers and flopped on the floor.

"When?" she giggled then, actually giggled.

"Well…" I stooped to pick up my sandwich. It was a good question. A week ago when Stewart and I had to run away from Imena, presumably because she was so pissed off that Soraya wasn't around, or that night, when the place was swarming with Japanese? Or since then? I hadn't seen or heard from her in days. Now here she was.

I shook my head and moved past her, and sat down in my chair. She moved away from me and stood with her back to the door.

"Listen," she said, looking down at her work boots. She was in her customary jeans and untucked, pastel-colored flannel work shirt; today it was yellow. Her bangs were long and her curls swung down over her face. I could see just a tip of shiny turned-up nose and red lips.

"We need help with Clara," she said. She was out of the hospital now and would recuperate at home for a few more days before coming into the lab, where she'd find her job completely changed. She wouldn't ever be allowed to get near the apes again, whether she wanted to or not.

"I can't imagine she'd want to," I said dully.

Soraya smiled a little and looked away. She was so officious, so polite. Something inside me started to pulse and hurt.

"Anyway, her doctor says she's got to go downtown every other day for physical therapy. Her father called me this morning from

Congo. He was very upset. Anyway she's got this shit car, and it broke down, and technically the lab is responsible for her injuries, so technically, we're responsible for getting her there. But nobody has time in their schedule to do it."

"Except me? Why me?" I knew I was whining now, but I was tired. Of course Clara's father would never have called her by her lab nickname, bestowed on her simply because it was easier for us to say, he would have called her Kalala, her given name. She deserved someone to take her to her doctor's appointments. She didn't deserve for Faraji to attack her. But she'd known what she was getting into. Hadn't she?

"She got the bandage off a few days ago, and she's got some nerve damage," Soraya held up her right hand, pointing to the fingers with her left.

"On these," she touched her right index and middle fingers, "she only lost the top digits —"

"Only?" I croaked, indignant for Clara/Kalala.

She smiled again. I hurt more.

"They're so stiff she can hardly use them. She just holds the whole arm at her side like it's completely damaged. She just wields it like a club. So she can't use a computer or a knife…her doctor wants her to have intensive physical therapy if she's going to use of any of the fingers on that hand again."

I stared at Soraya, wondering why the thought of driving Clara downtown every other day would make me angry. I was starting to lose explanations for what was happening. I still couldn't have told you what I'd done in the woods with her or how the memory of it was turning me into an insane person. I couldn't piece together why Imena seemed to want to kill Stewart and me in the woods, or why Marc and I were suddenly over and I couldn't speak to him, why Chloe was starting to feel like his daughter and not mine. Though I was desperate to, I couldn't have told you what it all meant. It was all starting to blur together, to fade out into a haze of confusion and exhaustion. I just knew that back in the summer, everything had seemed fine, and a few weeks later I'd completely lost track of what was going on.

Soraya came over and knelt by my chair. She put her hand on the armrest, over mine.

"I know it's hard," she looked down at the carpet again. "Your help is really important. I don't know what we'd do without you."

It was like a sales pep talk. From this woman whose mind worked like a maze, zipping and spinning in ways I couldn't fathom. Who was supposed to be so brilliant, who made me hurt so much. I was so confused now I felt like I was drowning. Before I thought about it, I asked her, "Where were you?" again.

"When?" She said.

I shook my head a little try to clear it. "Yesterday. Last week."

She furrowed her brow. Now she looked confused. "Why?"

I shook my head again. "Forget it," I told her.

Soraya talked about Clara a little then, how we wanted to make sure she was "happy." How angry her father had been, yelling at Soraya on the phone in a deep African drawl. How Clara so wanted to be closer to the apes, how Soraya felt she couldn't let her get any closer than she was now. How Clara really shouldn't ever have been allowed to be an ape caretaker.

"She came over here from Congo just to go in the cage with Faraji," I snapped. "And you won't let her do it?"

"I can't," Soraya shot back. "He attacked her. The university would shut me down."

She looked at me like I was a puppy.

"Even you know that, Deb."

Soraya went on about how Clara could sue — no, she could,

her father had money and they could afford lawyers here in the states with no problem — and how if she did that, it could force the whole lab to close down.

It occurred to me that people were suddenly constantly telling me, with their long faces and downcast eyes, how perilously close we were every day to the whole lab having to close down. This spot where we stood, this office, had been here for 20 years. Now, all of a sudden, all anybody ever talked about was how it could all melt away in a second.

I just kept shaking my head.

"I don't see what my taking her downtown every other day is going to do for her." I knew I sounded petulant, so I tried to keep the emotion out of my voice, and I realized I was holding my paper coffee cup over my face almost like a shield. But at the time I couldn't have told you why.

"I'm not sure I realized that was going to be a part of the job, is all," I told her. Now I felt like a brat. I turned my face away to look out the window.

Soraya reached up and took my chin and turned me back to face her. Then she put her hand on the right side of my face and put it into my hair. She watched her hand as she glided it through to the end near my shoulders, and she held the end of my hair and rubbed it a little in her fingertips. I stopped breathing. We were frozen like that for a second when Julian knocked on the door and said my name. Then Soraya got up and went to sit on the other chair, her backpack in her lap.

While Julian watched, Soraya told me I'd need to take Clara to the rehab center that morning at ten and then again on Monday at the same time. She asked if that was okay with me. I said it was. She got up and swung her backpack over her shoulder and walked out.

As the day was ending, Julian stopped by my office to say he and some other people were going out that night to Dugan's Pub for a beer, and did I want to come. I knew they went out almost every week, but they'd never invited me before. I thought they'd discuss research protocols or something, and I wouldn't have been able to follow the conversation anyway.

I felt fuzzy from the Soraya conversation, almost like my body was taking over for my heart and mind, sending me messages I couldn't come up with on my own. I thought how nice it might be to get dinner on the way home, surprise Chloe and Marc with it. I tried to envision stopping at the store, buying the food, bringing it through the front door. I couldn't figure out how it would all actually work, what Marc would say, what he would do. When Julian came by, I agreed to go out with them without giving the dinner surprise another thought. I called home and left a message for Marc, then got in my car and followed Julian to Dugan's.

Christine and Julian sat at a long table against the back wall of the bar. Emily and Sharla, two of Soraya's graduate students, sat with them. I took the seat next to Julian, Christine across the table from us on a bench against the wall. They were talking about Bill McComb, a primatologist from Emory who joined them for most of these gatherings and was on his way over. Almost as soon as I sat down and ordered a drink, he showed up. Clara came a few minutes after that, and we filled out the long table against the wall of the dark bar.

Bill had longish grey-blonde hair and hooded green eyes, and wore a worn-out green Koko t-shirt under a faded brown corduroy blazer. They introduced him to me. He looked tired. They introduced Emily and Sharla to me; I'd met them both briefly before at the lab, but they kept mostly to the back rooms, providing ape care and making meals. They'd have meetings with Soraya at her house or somewhere on campus away from the lab.

Everyone talked at once, and within minutes I didn't understand the conversation at all. They seemed to keep talking about big tracts of land, where they were and who had them. I didn't know why until Julian tapped me on the shoulder and leaned in close to me.

"You're new to this. You've only met the apes at their homes at the lab. The problem is" — he held up a finger to smile across the table at Emily, who was finishing up a joke about Faraji's weight, and take a sip of his beer. "The problem is that the grant funding pays for everything for the apes, even their food, and only for those apes who are actively involved in research projects. So apes like Malika, who's too old, and Joie, who's still really too young, there's no one to pay for their food. The university pays if we can talk them into it, and every year Soraya has to fight for it. Malika's in her late 30s now and…"

"How long do bonobos live?"

"Bonobos in captivity, I don't know. For chimpanzees, it's something like 50 years. Faraji's half that. So that means if we want to keep feeding him, he has to keep working. And he might not want to keep working. He might not be able to. So what the hell are we going to do with him?"

Bill was seated catty-cornered from me at the head of the table. He raised his beer glass to me.

"Apes just want to retire," he said.

That's why they were talking about land. Christine leaned across the table and told me it's what they talked about every week — where and how the apes would live in the future.

"We don't know," she said, shrugging and sipping her beer. "So we obsess about it."

I could envision her obsessing over it, worrying while she watched Faraji work on research trials, wondering while she

126

walked Imena through the woods.

"That's why I'm going to ditch the ape thing and work on dogs," Julian said quietly.

"Dogs?" I asked. "Why dogs?"

"Bill and I've been talking about dogs for awhile. Dogs are amazing. They build communities and they think and problem-solve. The apes can be so full of themselves. Dogs are just much easier to work with."

At the other end of the table, Emily was quickly finishing a second beer.

"And they're not quite so full of shit!" she laughed.

"Well," Christine said. "No, dogs aren't primadonnas, generally. And they don't live nearly as long as apes." She shrugged again, staring off down the table, pensive.

"And it's not as easy for them to kill you," Emily added. "And if they bite you, you clean it up and put a Band-Aid on it and you're done."

"We've been thinking about working with dogs for awhile," Julian said again. "We've been thinking about our next move, and we're thinking it's dogs. Bill and I maybe, in our own lab somewhere else…but yeah, dogs. There are border collies who know between 200 and 300 words." He was currently a postdoc in Soraya's lab, and if the university didn't offer him a professorship in the next few years, he would be slated to go elsewhere anyway.

"What would Soraya do if you left to work with dogs?" I wondered.

Julian just shrugged. I noticed Bill pursed his lips and looked away.

"Well," Christine said, "I don't imagine she'd switch to working with dogs."

"Yeah, I don't know what she'd do exactly." Julian said, and

I noticed he looked away too. I was starting to wonder about it when Bill sort of exploded.

"Soraya's out of her fucking mind," he spat out. The others just smiled.

I was thinking about her hand on my hair that morning and wondered if they could see it in my face.

Bill leaned in to me and continued, "Don't tell me you didn't know that."

"Bill, back off," Julian turned his attention back to us now. "Deb's new."

"Ah," Bill smiled. "So she doesn't know...yet."

He annoyed me.

"What do you want to tell me, Bill?" I asked him, looking him right in the eye, trying to be steely. Now he looked away. He wasn't willing to say any more and changed the subject.

I looked pointedly at Christine. In a low voice that traveled under Bill's new diatribe on ape sanctuaries, she said, "Soraya and Bill had a project together a couple of years ago. They were looking at ape community social structures. What the rules are among family members and among members of the same community. Who's in charge, what happens when the order is disrupted, that sort of thing."

She stopped.

"And?" I raised my eyebrows at her.

"And it blew up. Soraya either didn't do any of the data collection or she wouldn't share what she had with Bill. I never found out which it was. Neither did Bill. She wouldn't stick to the protocol. She said it was too taxing for Faraji and Imena..."

"It was a federally funded study," Christine finished. "She had to give the money back."

I didn't say anything. I was trying to figure it all out.

"She just…she just couldn't get it together I guess," Christine said. "She has kind of a weird idea about family."

"What do you mean, a weird idea about family?"

Now Bill wanted to come back to the subject of Soraya.

"Well, she has one of her own, for one thing," Bill said, quietly now. "Did she tell you that?"

He didn't wait for me to respond.

"She has a husband she left, a great guy, a scientist here in town, a friend of mine whom she tortured until he finally saw the light and let her go," Bill said. "She has a grown son she barely speaks to. Whom she abandoned when he was a kid."

I just looked at him. I wondered if they'd slept together.

"She's not a real…authority on family," he snickered. "She doesn't know anything about families. Her research focuses on ape families, but she has no idea what goes on in a real family. She hasn't produced a graduate student in years. Julian will be the first since the early 1990s. Did she tell you that? Did she tell you that all of her funding is threatened unless she gets her shit together?"

I stared into his obnoxious face. "No," I finally said, "she didn't tell me that."

Everyone around the table was silent for a second.

"I don't expect she would," Christine said quietly.

"That place is not a real lab," Bill said. "It's a French farce."

It got quiet again. At the other end of the table, Emily was telling Clara why she was leaving at the end of the semester. She kept her voice low but we could hear it plainly when we stopped talking.

"She won't sign off on my projects. She won't keep appointments with me. She won't let me work with the apes," she said, staring into her beer, not realizing our end of the table was listening now. "She's threatened by me. She's trying to stall me.

She just tells me to clean cages all day and make sure Faraji and Imena don't eat too much. I can't get anything fucking *done*."

Julian leaned in to me again, spoke directly into my ear, almost in a whisper.

"This is why we're talking about dogs," he said.

11

She probably doesn't even know it's haunted.

I let myself into the apartment after Dugan's, wanting to hold Chloe. Maybe we could be together for a little while on the couch, her asleep in my arms, I could think. The light in her bedroom was off. I was wearing boots and they made loud clacks on the hardwood floor that I didn't try to muffle as I walked past her door. She called out as I walked by, so I went in and lifted her out of her crib. She still wore diapers at night then, and I changed her. When I picked her up again, she held her arms out for her crib, angled her head and little body toward it, wanting to dive back in. So I didn't bother letting the crib railing down, just lifted her high in the air over it. Then, as I lowered her down onto her sheets, something went snap in my back.

For a second I couldn't straighten up at all. I propped myself up with my hands on Chloe's mattress while I let out a kind of silent yell, then put my hands on the railing, and very slowly pushed myself up to standing. Then I hobbled out of her room and to my bed. Marc was asleep and the lights were out.

The next morning he took Chloe to school and I very slowly, delicately made coffee. I discovered that if I cocked my right hip at an absurd angle, so that my toes dangled just off the ground, I could get around okay. If I set my right foot on the ground, an electric shock of pain shot from my lower back down my right leg and sparked out my toes. But I still went in to the lab.

Julian and Ardelle were standing at the desk and they watched me slowly creep in from my car. They thought I was joking around. By the time I got to the front door, they seemed to realize I was in pain, because I just looked at them helplessly and couldn't lean forward enough to open the door.

"What the hell happened to you? What, did you have a car accident on the way home last night? Jesus," Julian said, taking my elbow and helping me hop into the lobby.

I did look funny, and I started laughing with them. "I'm fine," I said.

"Yeah, you are so not fine. What happened?" he said.

"I don't know. I guess I hurt my back," I said. I started telling them how it happened and actually began to act out lifting Chloe over the crib rail, which made the pain in my lower back blow up again.

"No! Stop moving!" Ardelle said, coming around the desk to catch me as I nearly fell down. She picked up her radio and called Uba to come to the front desk.

"Why are you calling Uba?" Julian asked her.

"Uba can help Deb," Ardelle said plaintively. "He does massage. He can fix her back."

"I don't think so, Ardelle," I said, hobbling toward my office now. Julian was at my right side and Ardelle joined him on my left.

"You sure?" she said. We moved past her desk together and she put the radio down. I was breathing hard now, but I told her

I was sure.

Uba lived in and worked out of an old decrepit trailer on the lab grounds. Sometimes Soraya had meetings there, but it was dark and clammy and moldy. The windows were cracked and dirty. The entire northeast corner of the building sagged toward the ground.

"This is Uba," his voice boomed from on top of the desk. "Who is calling me?"

"Tell him never mind," I told Ardelle.

"Never mind," Ardelle said, but she had taken my keys and was unlocking my office door for me.

"No, tell him that over the radio," Julian laughed.

Ardelle left to go call Uba and Julian guided me into my chair.

"So you're fine," he said, as I sat gingerly down.

"Sure," I said.

He laughed at me then.

"You suck," he said. "You're so obviously messed up. You'd be the world's worst cancer patient. You'd be all, like, bald, 35 pounds, throwing up blood, sitting up in bed saying, 'I'm gonna beat this thing!'"

He was cracking me up so much I couldn't breathe.

"Alright then, if you're fine, I'm going to leave. Call me if you need help, you know, going to the bathroom or using the phone or whatever."

I was still laughing and I didn't answer. Laughing made a sick pain jump up from my hips and squeeze me around my lungs. Julian got to my door and then turned around.

"I forgot — we've got another visitor today. I was telling Ardelle when you came in."

"Oh my God, don't tell me it's somebody with a camera."

"No, this is a visiting scientist. A guy from Switzerland — or Denmark, it's one of those cold countries, I actually forget — Per Christensen is his name. Shouldn't be any trouble for you at all," he snickered again. "Though we can talk more about that later."

"What do you mean?" I asked him.

"Huh?"

"What do we have to talk more about? Is there something weird with this guy?"

"Per? No. He's very nice."

"Well then, what do you have to tell me about?"

"Nothing I'm going to tell you now. You got your hands full," he opened my office door and walked through it, then leaned back in. "But if you want to find out you could ask Uba while he's working on your back." Then he left.

"I am not going to that trailer!" I yelled after him.

Ardelle came in then.

"You really should. Uba is great. He's a healer."

I turned my chair around so that I faced my desk — very slowly. "Whatever," I said.

"Deb, come on now. You can barely walk. Uba can help you."

I waved her out and checked my email. Soraya had forwarded a note about Per Christensen, from the Anthropological Institutional Museum at the University of Zurich, who would be staying a few days. Per was going to be speaking on campus downtown and Soraya wanted to let me know I was invited.

There were so many subtexts to the email I didn't know where to start with them. I noticed Soraya didn't say where he was staying, and she usually had me coordinate where guests would stay, except with the Japanese. A nasty burning germ of jealousy started growing in the back of my head, spread through my stomach and clenched it into a knot. Was he staying with her?

Sleeping with her? What was he doing at the lab? Who the hell was he anyway?

So I'm supposed to be the gatekeeper, I thought, and nobody'd told me when Per was coming or where they were staying. Just like nobody had told me a truckful of Japanese were coming and going in the same night. They just blew through the place like a tornado and had fled by the next day. Even the duct tape they'd used to cover the video cables was gone.

I thought about how I needed more coffee, but the thought of getting up to get it was too daunting. I remembered that someone had told me once that if you have a back injury that you should lie flat on a hard surface like a floor. It hurt a lot to sit in the chair, so I lowered myself slowly and lay down, stretched out on the carpet. It took me several minutes of tiny, creeping movements to get down there. I lay there like a tick for ten minutes or so, resting my back and staring up at the ceiling.

Then I got bored and tried to get up to go get coffee. By then I couldn't move at all.

Ardelle came in to tell me something, not noticing until halfway through her sentence that I wasn't in the chair but on the floor, and she nearly stepped on my head.

"Now? Can I call him now?" She said.

"Okay," I said.

She picked up the phone and arranged the whole thing with Uba. I lay on the floor, my whole body burning and wanting to cry, listening to her talk about transporting me like I might make Chloe's arrangements for babysitting, if Marc and I ever went anywhere together anymore.

She helped me up off the floor and we made our way out of the building, and then we saw him on the road on the way to the trailer. Thin, tall, blonde all over with a blinding smile and wavy, honey hair. He actually wore a short-sleeved dress shirt with a pocket protector, like a geek badge on Adonis. The shirt hung off him like he was a model. He stopped and Ardelle introduced us. He leaned over to peer into my face like he was really concerned about my back.

"Deb, this is Per. Per, Deb."

I nodded at him. I was so jealous I wanted to hit him. Hit him and then lie down on the ground and cry for awhile. We moved slowly away, Ardelle practically holding me, steadying me while we inched along.

"I mean, come ON," she said under her breath once we moved out of earshot of him.

"What? I'm going as fast as I can," I spat out at her.

"No, not you, him," she giggled. "He is just so beautiful." She laughed and shook her head as she stared at my feet to make sure I didn't step on any rocks or roots and fall to the ground.

I tried to shake my head a little too, both of us staring at my feet to make sure I wouldn't fall, but it all hurt too much.

By the time I made it over to the trailer, leaning on Ardelle and cursing, Uba had set up a portable massage table in the middle of what passed for the living room. He didn't say anything, just opened the door wide so Ardelle and I could both fit through. He'd lit incense and the whole room smelled like he always did, like clean, warm dirt. Once we were both inside, he waived Ardelle away.

"I'll just pick you up and bring you to the table," he said to me, reaching down behind my back with his left arm.

"No, that's okay, I can make it," I warbled, grabbing a side table while my knees buckled.

He didn't react, just leaned down and picked me up and carried me to the table. It was like being picked up by a big, brown couch.

He took the weight off my feet, so my pain stopped immediately, until he set me gently down on the table, and another electric spark shot down and out my three middle toes on my right foot.

I sat there on the table, staring at my toes and wondering if I was going to react to every man I met the way I felt when I saw Per and Uba. Jealous, angry like a trapped raccoon, in so very much pain.

I didn't dare cry out in front of Uba. He saw my face screwed up in pain, and through my nearly clenched eyelids, I saw him see me. I felt ridiculous.

Ardelle was still in the room. She watched me wiggle a bit to get situated on the table.

"I can't believe we got her to come here," she chuckled at Uba.

Uba was moving around, setting things up. He had a couple of different kinds of essential oils, towels, things like that.

"Deb doesn't like me?" he said, his big, soft voice low, a hint of laughter in it.

"I don't think she likes the trailer," Ardelle said.

"I like you fine," I told Uba, picturing him holding Soraya. The jealousy was swallowing me from the toes up. Soon there wouldn't be enough left of me to form words.

"And she probably doesn't even know it's haunted," Uba said quietly.

"Oh, stop it," I told the two of them.

Ardelle believed in such things. She drove as quickly as she could down the road to the lab because, she'd told me once, she knew something lived in the woods on the sides of the road, and she could feel it watch her driving.

"Let's not talk about it now," Uba said. "You can leave us," he said to Ardelle.

Ardelle stepped over to me on the table first, leaned down and whispered, "There's something that lives under the trailer. I don't know what it is. It's a bad force. But while Uba's here he keeps it back. Don't ask me how, but it's afraid of Uba. So probably nothing bad wi —"

"Ardelle!" Uba spat at her.

"Okay, I'm going," she said, bustling around, going to the door, coming back. "You'll be fine, girl. You'll be just fine. I'll be back at my desk if you need me."

She left, quietly pulling shut the thin plastic-metal door.

It was mid-morning and bright outside but everything surrounding me was brown — Uba's t-shirt, Uba himself; the thin nasty trailer carpeting, the ancient canvas curtains blocking out most of the light from the window. One thin strip of sun shone in and actually glinted off the plain gold cross Uba wore around his neck. If I tell anyone that later, I thought, they'll think I made it up. I was ready to let Uba work on me to feel better, but I was used to the light, jokey camaraderie I had with most of the other staff of the lab by now, so I couldn't stop with it.

"So the trailer is haunted?" I asked him.

He set some oils on the table and faced me and sighed.

"Do you really want to talk about that now?" he said.

Actually, I really didn't.

"Will you tell me about it later?"

"Of course," he nodded. "Now let's see what's going on with you, okay?"

I told him what happened. I was lying flat on my back now, so I couldn't act it out. He closed his eyes and nodded. The story of how I got hurt didn't matter too much to him. He waited for me to finish, though, and he said:

"Well, what I'm going to do is this: I'm going to put my hands on you. Just for a minute. Just to see. Is that okay?"

"Sure," I said. I started to laugh for no reason, and I said, "I can't feel my toes."

"I'm sorry," he said. "I know it hurts."

That's all the talking he seemed to want to do. I'd wanted him to joke around with me the way everybody else did, but he was so earnest, and he really did seem to want to make me feel better, so I thought I'd better stop talking. My mind raced a little, casting about for something to think about other than the fact that I was hurt and about to get worked over by a big African guy I barely knew in a scary trailer. A man who'd kissed Soraya, who might love her. That sick thought lurked in my stomach, and it was there in my back, too.

I was definitely going to cry. I couldn't let him see it. I squeezed my eyes shut tight so he'd think it was just the pain.

Uba stood facing the table with his hands on my stomach and his eyes closed. It's my back, I wanted to tell him, but right away he started to frown.

"I can't help but notice that you're frowning," I said.

"Yes. I am," he said. He kept his eyes closed and pressed down a little with both hands. And frowned more. We stayed that way at least a minute, maybe more.

"I'm feeling some things here. There are a lot of things... going on with you, would you say?"

I didn't know what to tell him. Then he asked me turn over on to my stomach and put his hands under my right side to help tip me over. Turning over was excruciating and seemed to take about an hour. Once I was on my stomach, he put his hands on the small of my back and pressed down just a little. More minutes passed. I stared down at the carpet and wondered about the thing living under the floorboards.

Finally Uba sighed. "Miss Deborah...I'm feeling some things here."

"What things?" I said.

"There are a lot of different things. You...you think too much. You have a lot of...thoughts. For the moment, they're all balled up, right —" he pressed down on the small of my back just a bit — "right here."

He still wasn't making any sense, so I continued to stare at the carpet.

"I am not sure...how much you want to know about this," Uba said.

"Tell me everything," I told him, bitterly. "Preferably things that actually have to do with my back."

"You...I won't tell you this, Miss Deb, unless you really want to know. But you...you have a lot of fear and anger and...mostly a lot of fear. It feels like fear. It's a big, bad feeling. It's right here. It's here in your back. It's in a big ball right here under my hands, you see."

It was completely silly. "How can you tell all that?" I asked him.

"What is it you think a healer does, Miss Deb?" he asked quietly. "If I concentrate, if I put my hands on you and I don't let anything in my mind except you, here on the table in front of me, well, I can't not feel it. You're feeling pain your back, but your pain is only the symptom of all of these...other things."

I always have trouble when I come to this part of the story. I did start crying then, as quietly as possible. People want to know why I let Ardelle take me to see Uba in the trailer rather than calling my own doctor and getting a referral to an orthopedist. I don't know, really. Did he see Soraya there, in my thoughts? Did he love her too? I just stared at the dirty trailer floor.

"There is more," he said tentatively. "I can be more specific. If you want to know it."

There was a towel next to my face and I reached up and wiped my eyes with it.

"Go for it."

"You…don't feel good enough. You don't feel…worthy. Of being here with the apes, of having a lovely little daughter. Of your husband. You don't…you don't feel like you deserve these things. Is that right?"

I didn't say anything. I felt a slight pressure on my back, and then a lifting feeling, of weight taken away. For the moment there was no pain. It took my breath away. I kept trying to understand what was happening, but it was all going way too fast.

"If I am wrong, please say," Uba said quietly.

"I don't think you're wrong," I said after a moment. I was trying to figure out whether I'd ever even told Uba I had a daughter.

He squatted down on the floor next to me so that I could see his face. I stared at his teeth.

"Miss Deb, if I may. You must remember what to do when you have that feeling: sometimes you can talk to it. You say: what do you mean, not good enough? Not good enough for what? Not good enough to have a beautiful little daughter to love? Not good enough to be here with us at this lab? Not good enough to have a nice life in Atlanta?" He chuckled a little. "You are good enough for those things. You are good enough for everything."

I said nothing. I had nothing to say.

"It's as if you've put everything all together in a big…on a big stage," he went on. "It's so high up there, you don't feel like you can stay up. Every day you think you're going to fall. But you know, it's really…it's not one big stage, it's really little stages, isn't

141

it? Only a few steps up. Your job here with the apes and people who love you. That's a little stage. Being a mother. That's not so high up that you can't stay there. You're just fine up there. You can stay up. Do you see what I mean?"

At the time, I couldn't have told you if Uba was reaching into my heart and pulling out the truth, or if the thing under the trailer was sending evil thoughts through him, or if he and Ardelle concocted the whole thing just to laugh at me. It felt at that moment like any of those things were possible.

A few little dry leaves had drifted in through the open window. I stared hard at them for a minute and then put my whole face into the towel as the tears flowed out of me.

12

She can't hold a toothbrush with that hand anymore.

All I remember from that time is how much my back hurt. I remember inching my way along my life with one toe hanging off the ground. Chloe wanting me to pick her up, and my not being able to, standing there, both of us holding our arms out, both of us crying. The pain got slowly and steadily better over those weeks, and by the time it started to get colder out, I could touch the ball of my right foot to the ground. But it took a long, long time.

I remember, in excrutiating detail, trying to find Soraya around the lab without being able to get up and walk around and look for her. She nearly disappeared during those weeks. I'd ask Christine or Julian where she was and they'd just seen her, just had a meeting with her, just walked past her in the hallway, but they couldn't say where she was now. I couldn't go looking for her because I could barely make the trip from my car to my desk each morning. So I sat in my chair and looked out the window and did paperwork, willing her to come and find me, and she never did.

So I just sat and looked out the window for long afternoons at a time. It hit me on one of those afternoons why, almost the second I walked through the lab's front doors back in the spring, I'd started to shut Marc out. It was because ever since I'd met him, and through the years of our courting and marriage and Chloe, he'd been a sort of therapist to me. We were so alike, both so quiet and even and a little shy, that we'd fit together instantly when we met in college. There was no question we'd be together; it wasn't ever really discussed.

And I'd found, after a few years with Marc, that he often knew what was happening in my head before I felt it, let alone before I talked about it. When I was pregnant with Chloe, he'd bring me cookies in bed and hold my hand and nod and smile through mood swings and crying jags. Whenever he was pissed off about something he'd go for a walk in the woods and come back hours later, calm, refreshed, not even remembering what he'd been upset about. Not so much stoic as quiet and relaxed about his entire emotional life, and mine. So when I started feeling something for Soraya – when she hit me like a runaway truck – I knew I couldn't hide my feelings from him without hiding my whole self. It was why I never went home at night until I absolutely had to, buried my nose in a book and then turned to the wall. Two seconds of honest conversation and he would've had the whole thing figured out.

Now Soraya didn't want me, and Marc didn't either, and my body was broken and sore. Healing, sure, but slowly, haltingly, and not for any particular reason. No one could touch me and no one seemed to want to. Had what I felt for Soraya been love? Admiration? Some kind of fleeting physical tie, some cosmic connection? I couldn't tell anymore. She'd been the first woman for me and I knew now she'd be the last.

So did I still want to be married to Marc? I couldn't tell. We'd fallen into a business relationship. We spoke only when we had to now. We shared the same bed but didn't touch each other. My pain gave me the excuse to withdraw completely from him and I took it. I knew we should discuss what was happening but I had no words for it, and I knew he could go on like this forever, or until he found someone else. I thought if I bothered to look I might find clues that he'd already found someone.

I thought if I tried hard enough I could envision him leaving, and tried it once to see how I'd react. There was no reaction at all. The movie just didn't play in my head. I felt so frozen almost wanted it to happen so I could watch myself react. I wanted to be slapped back to life, shaken awake, but Marc would probably just let me sleep forever. He'd probably keep avoiding me in our apartment until we both got old, until Chloe went off to college, or one of us just forgot to come home one day. But then where would we go? All that was left was grey confusion, anger, longing I couldn't name that couldn't be assuaged now by either Marc or Soraya. I felt wooden, stupid, lumbering like an aging dog, staring out the window into the parking lot on ten-minute breaks from reconciling the credit card logs.

There was one particular stupefying weekend spent watching TV in bed while Marc took Chloe to visit his parents. When he left without even asking me if I wanted to go, packing up Chloe's books in a canvas bag without looking at me, I stared to wonder if he might somehow know more than I'd thought he did, if he'd found out about Soraya and me in the woods. But that was a long time ago now, nothing had happened since, probably nothing would ever happen again and there was no way he could find out about any of it, and anyway he would never say, so I'd never know.

The weekend he and Chloe went out of town, I spent watching Animal Planet in the apartment, the blinds drawn, the dog looking up at me as though the two of us were alone in the world. Clara — I'd started to think of her as Kalala, and lately, so had she — had been out of the hospital for a few weeks now, and called my cell phone on Sunday afternoon, her thick, dark African accent floating at me as if from oceans away. "This is Kalala. Please call me back," she'd said.

I hadn't. So when I got to my office door Monday morning, there she was, sitting at Ardelle's desk, looking at me like someone had died.

"I called you. You didn't call me back," she said.

I shrugged, which made my purse slide off my shoulder and knocked my keys out of my hand. I knelt down to get them, noticing in the same second both that Kalala was making no move to help me and that my name was typed on a 9x12 manilla envelope, the return address indicating it had come from the university research office downtown, that stood on the floor propped against my office door. My back groaned into position and started to sting.

"I think my father might sue the university," she said.

I picked up the keys and envelope and stood slowly and carefully upright, grabbing the doorknob to prop me up, then fell-slouched backward into the visitor's chair opposite Ardelle's desk. I blinked at her.

"Kalala. No." I stammered, in a wan haze from the pain. I wanted to get down on my knees and beg her, to make a show of it. But my back was made of such stiff, hard stone that even my thoughts hurt, and anyway that's not how a lab administrator should behave.

"Sorry," I said then, shaking my head, as though some errant sister of mine had ignored her call, not me. I waved my right arm toward my office door, sending a silver spike of pain down through my leg. "Let's go in here and we can talk."

She nodded and took my things while I unlocked my office door, and we stumbled in one after the other. She started talking before I got the key out of the door.

I found my chair and collapsed into it, and she sat in the visitor's chair. I got up and closed the door and locked it.

"You don't know," she began. "You don't know what goes on."

"Cla-Kalala, I only started here a few months ago," I said. "I'm sure I have no idea about a lot of things that go on here."

We were just getting started, but I was already rubbing my eyes with my palms. She looked measured, dry-eyed. She'd always been so calm, so relaxed and happy. Now she was a little scary. She took a deep breath and just looked at me.

"What do you mean your father is suing?" I said. "Let's start with that."

She shrugged.

"I don't know much about it. My father is very upset about my hand and wants me to come back to Kinshasa," she said. "He's the one who called the lawyer, not me."

I waited. She seemed to be waiting for me.

"What's your case? Who are you suing?" I finally ventured.

"Well," she put her hands back in her lap and looked down at them. "Soraya. This lab. The university." She looked up and frowned then, shook her head, as if it were already out of her hands.

"So...you're suing Soraya and the university. Because you got hurt?"

"Not just that. Not just that, Deb."

I waited again, but she seemed to think I knew what she was talking about, and I didn't really.

147

"Can you name three...things that are going on that you're upset about?" I ventured again. It was like we were staring at a car wreck, and she wanted me to point out the dead, to take her hand and explain the scene to her.

She started counting on her fingers, the ones on her right hand, that were half gone and still wrapped in dirty gauze.

"Let's see," she said, her voice growing stronger. "I cannot use this hand now, Deb. I cannot hold...my toothbrush with this hand anymore, Deb."

She took a breath, then: "I came here from Congo to work with Soraya and the apes. But she doesn't like me. So she won't let me near them."

Tears rolled down her face now. I wanted to scream at her to stop crying, to not sue, to not have ever been bitten, to not want to be near the apes. Because then things would just be so much easier.

"I just clean cages now, Deb. I didn't come here to clean cages."

I held up my hand to stop her.

"I'm sorry, I don't understand," I was consciously speaking as slowly as I could, calm therapist-speak, like Marc might. "Why do you want to go in with the apes if they mauled you?"

"If she let me go in with them they would know me," she started, talking fast now. "We would be equals. Not like she is with them. I would never threaten her. But now...I just clean. I'm ... a maid. They don't respect me."

I hadn't heard this line of reasoning before, and I took a minute to let it sink in. I loved the sound of her voice, so deep and smooth. I just couldn't stand what she was saying.

She shook her head and looked at the floor again then.

"You don't know, Deb," she said again. "You just don't know."

148

I winced then, and she saw me.

"What?" I said, shrugging. "What really goes on? How about some specifics?"

"Soraya and Uba," she began, patiently. "Soraya and the man from Denmark. She lets them go in. She treats the students so badly. She won't let them get enough of their work done so they can graduate. They're all leaving as soon as they can, did you know?"

I winced again, and decided I didn't care if she noted it or not.

"I heard Emily was leaving at the end of the semester. And Christine told me that ...Imena has been really difficult to deal with because she's pregnant." I sounded like an alcoholic at her own intervention.

She shook her head.

"No, Deb," she smiled then. "That's what I thought, too. When I first got here. When I first met Soraya and was so happy to be here to work with the apes. But no. We all have to leave. We can't stay here, Deb. We'll all get bitten if we stay."

She wiped her face with the back of her hand, but it wasn't enough; she wiped her eyes with the sleeve of her bleached-out t-shirt and dried her hands on her jeans. She smiled at me then. That's when I went over the edge.

"Who else? Who else is leaving?"

She shrugged.

"I don't know, Miss Deb. That's enough for me."

Now I was paddling water like a dog, trying to keep up with her.

"What about Uba?" I shot at her.

"Uba doesn't want to go back to Congo," she said dismissively. "Uba is making it so that he doesn't have to. Isn't he?" She raised her thick, dark eyebrows at me and I wanted to slap her.

"Ok. That doesn't explain why you want to sue the university, though," I said, momentarily proud of myself for trying to bring the conversation back onto some kind of track.

"Because she lets them in to the cages, Deb. She lets Julian and Uba into the ape enclosures. She lets them in. She won't let me."

"Uba goes in with the apes? Why?"

First Clara just cocked an eyebrow at me, but I ignored it and kept looking straight at her.

"Yes. Even though he's not supposed to," she said finally. "Only Soraya, Christine and Julian are allowed to actually go in with the apes. But she lets people in. She sneaks them in at night. As long as she really likes them. But she won't let me."

She looked me full in the face now.

"That's why Faraji bit me, Deb. Because he knows."

"He knows what?"

"Oh," she shook her head, annoyed. "I can't talk to you. You just don't want to know. I am looking at you. I am telling you. But you don't want to know. But I am telling you this: unless this stops someone else will get hurt. He will bite someone else. I promise you."

"Cla-Kalala," I began, like I was negotiating with someone on the ledge. "You understand, the university will shut this whole place down if you sue."

She looked me right in the eyes and nodded.

"You'll lose your job," I said thickly.

She rolled her eyes at me and gestured with her head out my office window, where her car was parked, right in the front.

"I'm going today. My car is packed already. I'm bringing my things to Uba to keep. My father sent me a ticket. I leave today. In just a few hours."

She started crying again then, just a little.

150

"I was so happy to come and work with someone like Soraya. Someone so famous, so respected. My family in Kinshasa, they think she is really the last hope for the bonobos in the U.S. But you know," and here she leaned forward, her hands in her lap and her eyes on mine. "I just can't stay here."

I hadn't been prepared for Kalala to actually make sense. I asked her if anyone else knew she was leaving, and she shook her head.

I watched her leave my office and walk out to her car. On the way, she stopped at Ardelle's desk and left her keys. Once she was gone I stepped out and looked to see that she'd also left her Taser. She'd never used it, had said she would never use one against any animal. She had it on her the whole time she was being pulled, grabbed, held to the chain link, bitten by the apes. She never reached for it.

I've thought back to that morning a lot, and now that it's all over, I look back and quiz myself to see if there wasn't anything, some shred of fear or at least dull concern, that Kalala had activated by telling me she was going to sue. I was more taken up by trying to figure out when Soraya would have had time to sneak off to see Per, the visiting scientist.

I watched Kalala get into her car and drive away, wondering if her father would actually sue, had actually started proceedings already, or whether she had told anybody else besides me about it. I realized I'd never see her again, that I was the only one she'd said goodbye to. But then, after she left, I seemed to have just put the whole thing out of my mind.

The envelope from downtown threatened to take up the entire rest of the day, anyway. It was a memo from the vice president for research. It looked pretty innocuous. It simply asked Soraya, via me, to forward a listing of all the costs of keeping a bonobo alive — food, shelter, medicine, supplies and salaries for the caretakers, broken down into a daily cost. I'd had to do similar computations for grant budget justifications. It was relatively easy, but Soraya kept a lot of the records in her office. I called her there, but she didn't answer. So I made do with what little information I had at hand for awhile, and then got gingerly up from my desk and made my slow march to her office.

The door to Soraya's office was ajar. She was there — like she'd been there the whole time, all the weeks I'd been looking for her. She and Christine sat side by side in straight-backed chairs, their backs to the door. Soraya's laptop sat on the desk in front of them, playing a video recording of the apes in their main enclosure, the one the researchers called the bedroom.

They were intent on watching and didn't notice me there, so I leaned against the doorjamb and watched too. In the video, Faraji played with Joie and the red ball while Imena and Malika sat together, grooming. Malika peered meditatively into Imena's hair, her fingers curled, poring over every inch of skin.

Soraya and Christine finally felt me watching and turned around. Soraya smiled and Christine looked upset, but didn't say anything.

"The research office wants to know how much per day it costs to keep an ape," I blurted out, as if it were an answer to the question why I'd been standing there, watching them. "You know, food, shelter, medicine, research supplies, salaries, cleaning stuff…"

Soraya knitted her brow. It looked like she was playing a private detective in a movie.

"Why? They've never asked for that before."

I opened my mouth to tell her I didn't know, when a movement at the window made me stop. The window was high up on the wall, about four feet long but only about a foot tall. The only thing you could really see out of it was the lowest canopy of the pines right outside Soraya's office. Suddenly the heads of four men I'd never seen before went very quickly by, followed by Julian.

Christine and Soraya saw me looking and swiveled back around in their seats. Soraya's eyes went wide and Christine said, "what the hell —" in a growl, like a cat. The men's heads floated past the window toward the back of the building. Soraya stood up then, grabbing the back of her chair. "Where is Faraji? Where is Imena?"

Christine didn't answer her. She grabbed her radio and keys off Soraya's desk and ran out of the office and down the hall toward the back door. Soraya ran out too, but went the other way, toward the door leading to the apes' bedroom. I knew I wouldn't be allowed to go into the ape enclosure so I followed Christine.

When I got outside, Christine was striding up to the men, who stood shoulder to shoulder, looking into the ape enclosure. All four of them wore expensive-looking suits. Your visiting scientists, your London *Sunday Times* photographers — they all tended to wear jeans, t-shirts, hiking boots when they came out to the lab. These looked like government men from Europe, which is, in fact, what they turned out to be.

Once I got up to them and stood next to Christine, Julian made introductions. The men were from the Max Planck Institute in Liepzig, he explained. They all had long names that started with Dr. that I don't remember now. Each nodded at Christine and me as they were introduced, and as Julian said their names, Christine straightened and turned toward them. It was clear she didn't know them personally, but had heard of them. You could tell she knew who they were and was trying to afford them some respect.

Julian didn't say why they were there. I found out later they were in town for a scientific meeting with Terry Oakley from the zoo, who had suggested they drop in and say hello to Soraya and the apes. I found out later that Soraya had a years-long feud with one of them, who had denounced her work before a packed house at the New York Academy of Sciences a decade before. I found out that he'd made it his career publishing work that decried the ability of any ape to master language and culture, who consistently wrote that the ability to form language is distinctly human. Soraya had hated him for years.

A low growl came from the doorway leading from the apes' bedroom to their outdoor enclosure. We all spun around to see Soraya crouched there, inching her way outside. I expected her to stand up once she got outside, but she didn't. She kept crouching, crawling her way out, and her knuckles dragged on the ground. She was an ape. She moved toward Faraji, who I finally focused on now.

We all did. He sat in the corner of the enclosure, himself in a defensive crouch. When we all turned to look at him, he started pant-hooting. It started low and growly, then got increasingly loud, so terribly, incredibly loud that it blocked out everything else. I thought it was some kind of combination warning/greeting but it didn't stop. Christine and I put our hands over our ears. Soraya scuttled over to his side. She didn't greet the men or say anything to us. She looked frightened for a second, and then she seemed to become an ape. She crouched beside Faraji and started pant-hooting, yelling in warning at the men.

"SHE'S TRYING TO —" Christine was yelling over the hooting and screaming, trying to explain to the men what was happening, but they couldn't hear her. They'd stepped backward off the concrete walkway into the grass, and here and there they winced and turned away, because now Faraji was throwing pine bark through the chain link at them. The smell told me he might also be throwing his own shit.

"I THINK SHE'S TRYING TO -- " warn them, she told

me later, because Faraji didn't have a girlfriend and was very threatened by men in suits who hadn't been previously introduced, and preferably by Soraya herself. She said Soraya must have felt threatened too, being next to Faraji in the ape enclosure when he was yelling, thinking about getting violent. She said Soraya had to show Faraji she was on his side, not on the side of these rude visitors.

But none of us could hear Christine at the time, and there was so much screaming my ears started throbbing, and then Soraya rushed the chain link and threw herself on it screaming, throwing pine bark, screaming, screaming, her face full of hate, her arms spread wide and her hands clenched on the chain link, three feet off the ground, hooting and screaming.

Julian and Christine and I stood gape-mouthed as the men turned around the way they came, their expensive-suited arms held over their heads to protect themselves from the flying shit and pine bark, and left without another word.

13

She lacks self-confidence.

As it turned out, information on the amount of money it took to keep an ape alive was only the first thing they wanted downtown. They called on a Tuesday, wanting me to bring the information to a meeting the next morning. Soraya had slinked out of the ape enclosure after scaring off the men from the Max Planck Institute and hadn't been seen around the lab since. So it was a simple matter to let myself into her office, looking around for cost data and trying to look at nothing else, so that I could fill out the form to have it ready for them.

I allowed myself only about 20 minutes to get the data, fully ready for Soraya to burst in at any time. I'd stand up and go to the door, explaining that I was just looking for receipts and purchase logs, that I hated being in her space when she wasn't there, but that they wanted information downtown and I just had to. I shivered under the air conditioning in her chair, flipping through the notebooks, hunting down files and receipts she was supposed to have filed with me in the first place.

What would she say if she found me in her chair? Wouldn't she be startled? Would she come over and sit down and chat with me, and things would be like they'd been a month ago? Would she be ashamed that just a few days ago I'd seen her pelt ape shit at the scientists?

Papers lay everywhere on her desk, overlapping, forming bridges with books over other papers and creating tiny spaces I poked into with a pencil so that I didn't have to move anything. I peered under paper corners, lifting them up to look underneath. Most of it was typewritten pages from the research office or the university's Institutional Animal Care and Use Committee, which everybody called by its ugly acronym, IACUC. I picked up a thick stack with the National Institutes of Health seal on top, thinking it might have to do with one of the grants and might give me some numbers. Underneath it was a legal pad covered with Soraya's handwriting, small, neat and girly cursive. At the top of the first page was my name.

I put my pencil down and pushed the chair back from the desk. My chest felt hollow, sucked out. They were always telling us to breathe in those yoga classes I never had time for anymore, breathe, breathe in life and health. I glanced over my shoulder at the windows to make sure no one was there, and took the deepest breath I could force into my dry little chest.

If it was a letter to me, I should wait until she was ready to give it to me. But if I went back and looked at just the beginning, only the opening, it would tell me so much. I wouldn't need to look at the whole page, covered with her writing. I could just look at the beginning.

I looked around the room again. The fact that I'd found the letter made it seem inevitable that someone would burst in. I was sure that if I actually touched the legal pad, the room would be full of people in two seconds. Then I touched it anyway.

It wasn't a letter. It was research notes.

— 6/26: Pretty. Lacking self-confidence. Moves around as she expects someone might call her on all she doesn't know, or hit her. Seems afraid of everything. Likes me. Likes being with me, sitting together. Her home life is not good. Doesn't seem to like her husband very much. Has a child she never talks about. Doesn't have a lot of self knowledge. Is childlike almost to childish. Does the numbers well — a good administrative type, the lab needs —

I was so into reading it that I didn't hear Julian open the door and peer in. I jumped out of Soraya's chair.

"I was looking —"

"Relax, Deb, I just needed a book. It's fine," he crossed the room quickly, and pulled down a binder from a dusty wooden shelf under the window. He looked back over his shoulder at me. "Really. We all have to sneak in here to look for missing data once in awhile. It's like she eats it."

I chuckled a little, feeling sick. I wanted to ask him if he'd ever found a file on himself in her office. But apart from the one on me, I didn't see any other handwritten notes on anyone else. Julian had been here for years, though. Had she made notes on him when he first started? Had she taken him outside at night, when he was a fresh, young student, probably in love with her too? Had they had sex? Maybe those notes, a couple of years old now, had moved from the desktop to one of the file cabinets in her office, covered with African blankets. Were they all filled with notes of us, or was I special?

I sat there thinking all of this while Julian got the book he wanted and left. I hid the legal pad under some other files. I tried to cover it completely, but it was though I could still smell it under there. After a few minutes I just left, backing out of the room without the data I needed, and went and sat in my office, looking out the window for the rest of the afternoon.

I wore my only suit the next morning, going straight from our apartment to the downtown campus to be in the research office conference room at 9 a.m. My suit was blue pin-stripe and a little short for me, but the jacket was fitted and attractive. I felt pretty good in it, if misplaced. I put on lipstick that morning, since that's what you do when you put on a suit and go downtown. When I dressed in jeans and button-down shirts for the lab, lipstick always seemed silly. Soraya often wore it though — the students said when she had it on it was a good quick way to tell at a glance whether she felt more human on that particular day, or more like an ape.

I put on a pinkish-melon lipstick that seemed to make my hair even lighter, more champagne than butter, and thought about how she'd looked the day the scientists came. I could tell she'd gotten herself together a bit that morning, brushed her curly hair, stained her lips a dark red and maybe even brushed on a bit of mascara. But by the time she set upon the chain link later that day, her face was dirty, her lips a cold purple-grey. Goose-bumps rose from her arms as she grabbed handfuls of shit and pine bark and threw it through the fence.

I walked through the door marked Richard Dorn, Vice President for Research, and into his conference room. I held the manila envelope with the care data in front of me, moving to give it to Dot, who said she was his assistant. She had creamy white hair in a beehive, and seemingly even whiter skin. She wore a tight blue suit and her glasses dangled from a chain around her neck.

"What's this?" she said, pleasantly enough.

"It's the data Dr. Dorn asked for," I said, sitting and attempting to make myself comfortable in the cushy conference room chair.

"His memo asking for amounts for daily ape care."

"Oh," she said, and looked around. "Okay. I'll go and give that to him. You didn't have to bring it, that's fine." She got up and took the envelope over to a side table and set it down.

Dorn hadn't yet entered the room, and Dot seemed like if I asked her about what the hell I was doing there, she might tell me.

"So...you won't need the data this morning, for our meeting?" I ventured after a minute. I smiled at her, as if to say, please level with me, let me know what's going on before he comes in here.

She sat down across from me, with an air of just taking a load off for a second, as though she didn't intend to sit through our meeting.

"No, dear, we don't need that just now." She was fidgeting with her glasses on the chain.

"Okay," I said. I shrugged and looked her right in the eye. I felt drunk almost, as though I was ready for anything, and had better be. "What then?"

Could they have already heard about what happened with the guys from the Max Planck Institute?

She just smiled at me for a second, and when she opened her mouth to speak, Dr. Dorn came in through his open office door. I'd met him only very briefly when I came to sign my work contract, and he'd said basically nothing to me then. He was tall in a powder blue suit, almost gangly, with thin blonde hair and a long, pale, sun-damaged face patchy with pink scar tissue. He sat down and politely stretched a smile across his lips.

Dot leaned forward conspiratorially.

"I do like your suit," she said. Then she got up and left.

Dr. Dorn made small talk for a few minutes, asked me how I was doing, about how we needed the rain, silly things. Finally I was able to bring up the data in the envelope on the side table.

"I just wanted you to know I did my best — we did our best — at the lab, to get that information for you," I told him. "It can be a little difficult to come down to a daily rate for ape care because it fluctuates so much. I mean, it can vary based on diet, or vet bills, or items that Sor —Dr. Ruhl buys for research projects, and I wasn't sure what —"

"Well, and you've not been there long," he said, dismissively, waving his hand a bit.

"Well, that's true, I haven't, but that's not really the problem. It really does fluctuate a lot. There are so many —"

Now he really did dismiss it. He cut me off, nodding.

"Yes, yes, that's fine. I'm afraid, though, that we're really beyond all that at this point. You've been working with the grant documents. You know that the end date for Soraya's main grant is November 30."

I nodded, but slowly.

"Sure…but I noticed that it's a multi-year grant that's been running for almost ten years, and it ends every year on that date, and every year it's renewed."

He nodded impatiently.

"Except this year."

I had no idea what to say, just raised my eyebrows at him a bit. He seemed to raise his eyebrows back, but maybe I imagined it, I couldn't tell.

"The grant will not be renewed this year. We got the e-mail yesterday."

"So…" I traced a trail in the furniture polish residue on the table with my finger.

He nodded.

"If you're guessing this means the lab will need to close, you guessed right."

I looked up at him. I hadn't guessed any such thing. I'd guessed that the research office was going to pony up the missing money from their overhead — I knew they charged something like 40 percent on top of every grant they administered. For a second I'd been thinking, tracing little curlicues with my pinky fingernail on the table, that he might start into a firm but fair lecture about how things needed to change at Soraya's lab, how we needed to buckle down and be better about the rules. Not that we would need to close.

I couldn't even form a question in response. I just stared at him. Finally I mustered, "I don't understand." I shook my head. I felt like the child Soraya had written about in her notes on me, flushed and petulant. "I just got there."

He nodded quickly. He seemed to be trying to reassure me using only his head.

"We were afraid things might go down this way when we sent you out to the lab. Ape labs are expensive. Apes bite people. The insurance costs are astronomical. Overhead doesn't begin to cover it. And then the granting agency started making noises last year about some inappropriate charges to the preapproved budget. Well, of course, we just can't have that. We sent notices to Soraya but we never got any response, and when we asked her to come down here for meetings she didn't come. Then —"

He did keep talking, but nothing past the first sentence really registered. I waited for him to take a breath, then I started to shake my head very slowly again. I held up my hand to try to get him to slow down. It took concentrating hard to look up at him and ask, "Sorry? You said sent me. You sent me?"

He took up with the nodding again.

"Sure. Your supervisor in PR said you were conscientious, liked working with big research projects, were detail-oriented. We thought you could give us a little feedback as to how things were going out there."

"I'm a spy?" I just squinted and peered at him. I thought spies knew they were spies. I remembered when Julian had called me the lab's buffer, and I looked at him perplexed, like everyone knew what I was supposed to be doing but me.

He winced a little and shrugged.

"No, you're not a spy, but we did envision you as a liaison between the lab and the university. Someone who could keep the money straight out there, and send news back to us.

"Now that the lab will be closing, there's going to be a lot for you to do in the next few months. Some faculty are going to need to move to other places within the department. A few of the graduate students may ask to be reassigned, if they don't leave. A few have already contacted me about it. Then there's a lot of back-end accounting that needs to be done for the funding agency. When all that's done, somewhere after the first of the year, we'll have a position here in Contracts and Grants you might want to look at, when one of our analysts goes on maternity leave."

I was still stuck on the spy thing. I just looked at him. He'd said, "when we sent you…." I thought Soraya had hand-picked me.

"I thought —" I said and then stopped, helpless.

"Look, it was obvious they needed help out there. We thought that if we sent you, you could help keep us abreast of developments, is all. And that's going to be even more important now that the lab is closing."

He started talking then about disposal of the animals. I jumped when he mentioned Imena and Faraji and Joie. All this time I'd been envisioning what the people would do if the lab closed. How Ardelle and Christine and Uba and Kalala would need to find new jobs. Wait — Kalala was already gone.

But the bigger point, Dorn's point, was that when the lab closed, all the apes would be homeless.

He went on for another little while, and it registered with me, finally, that he was saying it might take weeks or months to find a suitable place for the apes to go. There were sanctuaries scattered across the country, though, so — he kept nodding, it was very distracting — surely arrangements could be made without too much trouble. Then he seemed to realize I wasn't really taking it all in, so he reached forward and patted my hand.

"Next week. We'll work on mapping out a plan on our end. You'll come in next week and we'll work out some details. We just wanted you to be aware of what's coming down the pike."

I looked at him.

"What happens to Soraya?" I said.

That's when he leaned forward and pushed himself up from the table.

"Well. Obviously we'll need to discuss that with her."

But he didn't leave the room. He went over to the window and looked out for a minute. Then he turned to look at me and came back over and sat down where he had been.

"It's a shame, I know," he said. "Soraya has been at this university for 20 years. Brilliant researcher. Built that place from the ground up. She created it. Wrote the grant proposals and went up to DC and won them over. Years and years of work."

He looked past me now, over my shoulder.

"But the entire project's been going downhill for years. And the liability has gotten so out of control. People getting bitten... students leaving, threatening to sue..."

He waved it away with his hands.

"We just can't have it anymore. There's nothing more to be done, really," he said, looking at me now.

"Why are you telling me this part?" I said, blurting it out. Soraya had created the lab, was its queen. Now she was set to fall. In front of me, the apes, the students, the staff.

Dr. Dorn nodded. It seemed to be all he could physically do. He hiked up his eyebrows as he told me: "You asked."

He patted the conference table once with his hand and then pushed himself up and out of the chair. The meeting was over.

I'm sure I must have gotten up and left the room, maybe even shook his hand, but all I remember now is the shiny surface of the conference table, how I felt like a car had crashed into the room and all I could do was stare at the crumpled cab.

14

She was nutty. She was screaming.

I drove back to the lab in a trance. Back before Chloe, back when I had time for those yoga classes that resurfaced to remind me to breathe when I was crouching in Soraya's office waiting for her to burst in on me, I'd learned a surefire way to calm down when I was stressed out: Count backwards from 108, and make every number a breath. 108 was a hallowed number, offered by my yoga teacher as the quickest way to enlightenment. She wore a mala, a string of 108 beads, around her neck. She sat cross-legged on a carpet dais as if floating just above us, long wavy blonde-streaked hair falling across a turned-up, sunburned nose, eyes closed and smiling heavenward, touching each bead between her thumb and index finger as she counted.

I angled out of the tight downtown parking lot, swerving to avoid concrete poles smeared with the paint of a thousand cars wrenched up against them, and started counting. You were supposed to picture the numbers, see the breath, it was supposed to clear your mind. But for me the thoughts popped up with the numbers like whack-a-mole. 108: Soraya told me she had picked me herself to come out to the lab and help them with PR. Didn't she?

107 and remember to breathe: I'm at my desk downtown at the beginning of summer. The phone rings and it's actually Christine asking to come out to the lab to meet Soraya, giving me directions. I'd always envisioned Soraya standing over her as she made the call, so in need of my help that she wanted to make sure Christine reached me on the first try. I'd dismissed the thought that it was actually someone else on the phone and had begun to believe Soraya had called. Now I wonder if Soraya even knew about me at all before I showed up for my interview. I flushed hot, sliding through stop signs, driving fast. Everybody working behind the scenes had probably set the whole thing up for Dr. Dorn before Soraya even knew my name.

106. He sent me out there to keep things under control, and it didn't matter that I didn't know it, or that I hadn't been given any time to get much of anything done. In the end it was the missed grant deadlines and unauthorized credit card charges that would bring the lab down, not ape escapes or lawsuits by mauled ex-employees or disrepute in the international scientific community.

105 and I was completely forgetting to breathe, at least Dr. Dorn had told me I didn't have to break the news to anyone at the lab. He had meetings scheduled with Christine and Julian over the next couple of days. He didn't want to get into when and where or how he'd get the news to Soraya. At first I thought it was because she was faculty and we were staff; meetings between faculty and the vice presidents had so far seemed so secret, so rarified, the details strictly guarded. But no, it was probably just because she wasn't taking his calls. Because she wasn't really taking any calls, answering any emails, or having any conversations with people

she wasn't sleeping with, or apes.

104. I hadn't even asked about the apes. I was so focused on the people. Had Dr. Dorn noticed that? Fuck him if he did. But, 103, how ridiculous that I had been the fumbling front-woman all this time, never even knowing I was a spy. I who wondered where Ardelle would get a new job before I thought to ask about where the apes would live. The grant paid for their food, their vet bills, the blankets that covered the floor of their enclosures. What would Soraya do, try to take them back with her to her house?

102 and where would Soraya go? Would they ship her off with the apes or try to keep her around in her some other smaller lab, conducting experiments with monkeys? Or would they offer her a take it or leave it-type teaching position downtown? What would Soraya do away from her woods? She wouldn't go. I was sure of it.

I only got to 101. I felt her hand on my chest again. Suddenly it felt like she was there with me as I drove. I tallied up all the things I wanted to say to her but couldn't over the last weeks. It had been so completely impossible to find her, to be alone with her. I held the steering wheel like I was drowning. The things I needed to say to her would fill up a big bag. I'd never know which to pull out first, not even now. I was breathing fast and hard, shallow, a panting dog. Thinking about her felt like the first two seconds underwater when you first see that you're not going to able to make it to the surface in time. Light but still sinking.

I forgot about counting and focused on slowing my breathing down, pretending I had her hand on my breastbone again, pressing gently to calm me. Still in my trance, I drove the rest of the way to the lab, pressing my numbers in at the gate like a robot, staring straight ahead.

It was about to storm, and the light disappeared as I turned down the lab's main road, under its dark canopy of trees. I could smell the tarmac steaming at the first drops of rain. I hunched over in my little car, wondering what I would say to anyone. I thought of going to visit the apes, of looking through the windows at them and talking to them about treats, feeling like an impostor, a thief, the first and so far only one to know that life as they knew it was going to end soon.

Then, about a half-mile in on my left, the woods on the side of the road had a huge hole ripped out of them. It was probably eight feet wide and ten feet tall, opening up the swath to sunlight that poured down as into an empty bowl. Broken sticks that used to be small pines stuck up out of the ground. Bigger trees were pulled up, dead, lying on top of one another. Man-sized mushroom clouds of red dirt stood nearly as tall as me, azalea bushes sticking out sideways, their tiny pink and bridal white blooms hanging down at right angles, still fresh. I stopped the car and got out, leaned against my door, staring, gape-mouthed. Earth-mover tire tracks with more carnage on either side zigzagged back through the woods as far as I could see.

Julian pulled up in the Tahoe, coming from the main building. He stopped in front of my car and got out. I just kept staring at him. He started to talk to me then, and but for a second I couldn't understand what he was saying, I just watched his lips move out of time with what was happening, like a character in a Japanese monster movie. Slowly I realized that he wasn't talking about the carnage in the woods. That's why it didn't make any sense to me. He wanted to know if I'd seen Soraya on my way in.

"The last time anybody saw her she was on the earth mover. She rented it. They dropped it off this morning."

"So," I waved my hands in the general direction of the dead foliage. "Soraya? Did this?"

Julian nodded.

"She's been talking to Per about building an ape sanctuary. She was supposed to clear out just a little bit of land so they could build some new enclosures. It was supposed to be right behind the main building. This…." He pointed at the carnage now too. "I don't know what the hell this is."

"She didn't mean to clear this land? What did she do, go crazy with the earth mover?" I said it in falsetto, feeling like I was starting to lose it now. Julian stared at the dying azaleas and just nodded.

"She had a huge monster fight with Christine this morning. Well, actually Christine and Imena and Faraji and Malika. They were all screaming. It was insane. You missed a big one, Deb."

Now I stared hard at Julian.

"What was the fight about?"

"I don't understand it completely. Well — that's not true. Yes I do. I just don't want to because it's completely stupid." He looked off into the woods. It felt like we were talking about a human family and he was about to tell me about hormonal fights and women's hurt feelings. He seemed embarrassed. "Soraya said she was very angry at Malika. That Malika had gone against her wishes and brought the babies where Soraya didn't want them."

It didn't make a whole lot of sense, but neither had anything for a couple of weeks. "How'd Christine and Imena and Faraji get involved?"

"Deb, Soraya was nutty. She was screaming. Christine told her to calm down and so she started screaming at Christine. Faraji and Imena started hooting and running around. Finally she got the hell out of there, went off somewhere, apparently on the goddamned earth mover, and it took me an hour to get the rest of them calmed down. I gave Christine a valium and told her to go home." He looked at the ground now. "She's really over it, Deb."

"Christine?"

"Yes. Christine…Where were you? Downtown for something?"

I felt like I'd been stealing. I stared off down the path left by the earth mover and tried to forget to answer him.

"Where'd she learn to drive one of those things anyway?"

"I don't know. Maybe Per. They're coming back to pick it up tomorrow. God forbid she should stick to the plan, clear the little area behind the main building that we all agreed on. I hope she hasn't dumped it into the river."

I felt the hairs on the back of my neck stand up.

"Let's go look for her," I said urgently, starting down the crazy path she'd left, looking back over my shoulder at him.

"That's what I was doing when I ran into you," he answered, starting to come after me, then stopping and looking back. "What about our vehicles?"

I waved him off. "They're fine. Let's just go. Let's find her."

If he thought there was anything weird about my being so hot to find Soraya he didn't say anything about it. We picked our way through about six feet of upturned red dirt before I realized I was still in my suit and heels. Again, if he noticed he said nothing. It gave me license to feel even crazier, my heels sinking into the dirt, my suit sucking up the moisture in the air. He held back dying branches so they wouldn't scratch me. My guilt at not telling him what I knew made me sick.

"Do you want to know what I think is going on?" Julian asked me, making my heart pound.

"Sure," I told him, pretending to concentrate on not falling down.

"The family structure is breaking down. With the apes. Malika is the mother figure. She's on the top of the food chain. Now Soraya is challenging that. She wants to be on top. She took the babies away," he was working hard to clear the brush away so we could walk, and he had to stop and catch his breath. I stopped and looked at him.

"That's really what she's doing?"

He nodded. "That's why Malika freaked out. That's why Christine had to get involved. Soraya took the babies and locked them up in the other building. She sent Uba to go and feed them, so they're fine, of course. But Malika doesn't know that."

Christine didn't have children of her own yet, but somehow she knew a lot more about what to do and not to do than either Soraya or me. Julian kept talking.

"And now we get to deal with this," he gestured to the makeshift path, which did seem now to go all the way to the river. "Just so she can show off for this Per guy. So she can show him her grand vision for an ape sanctuary."

Now we could hear the earth mover in the distance. We stood and waited as it came closer, and then as it re-entered the path about 50 feet ahead. Julian called out to Soraya, driving the thing, eight feet up in the air, her hair in a ponytail and a baseball cap, in a sweatshirt and jeans. I don't think she could hear him, but she waved. Then she turned, rocking gently as the thing climbed over a mini-mountain of red earth, lifted the huge yellow gaping bucket with its jagged dinosaur teeth, and ripped a couple pines out by the roots.

16

You will not challenge me.

It was two weeks before Dr. Dorn pulled Julian and Christine into his office to talk about closing the lab, so I had to wait around feeling like a louse, my stomach crawling like it had bugs in it, every day. One Thursday afternoon, Christine and I sat in my office, eating ice cream.

"Emergency," came Julian's low staccato. "Malika is out."

You would expect the static of the dozen radios we had stashed all over our 55-acre campus, but only silence followed.

Christine stood up to look out my window and grabbed for her radio.

"Julian, this is Christine….How out is she?" There was always the possibility she'd only gotten to an outer enclosure, behind just one locked chain link gate rather than the much safer two or three. Then we'd have a few tense minutes waiting for her to be escorted back in, but not much else — like Yi-ku had when he'd gotten out over the summer.

Another second followed and I looked around for the gun and the tasers. We really should've had those things taped to the wall. Then the static of Julian's radio for a few seconds, then some more silence.

Then, over the radio: *"Out* out," Julian said. "Gone."

Christine ran out my office door. I slammed it, locked it, paced my office three times, sat down, stood back up, reached for the phone, hung it up again without dialing 911, went to the door, unlocked it, and went to stand by Ardelle's desk. She had that wide-eyed look again. She looked like somebody'd slapped her. She was reaching for the phone to dial 911. I told her to put down the phone. She put it down. She got up and went to the door. "You better sit down," I told her. Then we both paced the reception area waving our hands around in front of us like the Three Stooges.

Then I thought, wait a minute. He said Malika was out. What does Malika want out for? In nearly 30 years of capitivity, she'd never tried to escape or bitten anyone. It was the research stars — Faraji, Imena, Yi-ku — who had the hair-trigger personalities. Malika wasn't a research ape, she was just an ape. She took care of the kids all day. She was never on TV or had her name in the newspaper. She was just Mommy. That's when I remembered my conversation with Julian the day before.

Twenty minutes passed and my ice cream melted in my office while Ardelle and I paced the reception area, scanning the parking lot for Malika. Julian called from over the radio. He had no idea where she was. This was not the way we'd practiced for escapes.

Then suddenly, there was Malika. Ardelle spotted her at the far right edge of the yard, just beyond the parking lot. She was hunched over, moving slowly. She looked old. Her long black hair was parted in the middle of her head, her part glinting in the sun. Hunched over, moving slowly and deliberately toward the front door. She'd stand upright and take a few steps toward us on her hind legs, then plunk back down on all fours, running out of energy.

Julian was still talking on the radio. Ardelle took mine and quietly radioed to him that we could see Malika in the front yard.

She was moving slowly, but there was no question now that she was coming toward us.

Then so was Soraya. Suddenly she was in the reception area with Ardelle and I. She was yelling. I couldn't make out what she was saying though, because my cell phone rang at that moment and it was Christine.

"Well, we know what happened now," she said.

"Why? What?" I didn't realize until then that I'd been yelling too, and my voice reverberated off the windows and the tile floor.

"This morning. Soraya took the babies over to the other building. She said she had to punish Malika for the fight the other day. Soraya took the babies. Malika's been screaming all day long. And now look."

I was still holding my cell phone when Soraya turned it up a notch. She started yammering at Ardelle and me as if we were Malika. She was dirty and she paced the shiny tile floor. There were leaves in her hair.

I could see it then, what everyone had been trying to tell me. What Julian, Christine and Dr. Dorn had been driving at. What she'd sent me a clear signal of herself just yesterday, waving from the driver's seat of the front loader. It was true. She was losing it.

"You don't understand. You're constantly trying to undermine me, constantly," she said under her breath now, pacing, lecturing mostly to her own shoes. "I told you. I told you….You don't mind me, I take the babies and I move them to where I can watch them until you do mind me."

Soraya looked up and stared right through me, talking to Malika like she was standing there in the room with us. Her eyes were rimmed with red and she smelled, like she'd been outside a long time, rolling in warm dirt.

"I am the mommy. I AM. And you will not challenge me," she said now, looking right at me as if she thought I might be Malika. Her body bent forward like she was getting ready to vault over Ardelle's desk. "You will not. I'm not gonna have it."

I was still on my cell phone and Christine was on the line, listening. Probably holding up her own cell phone in the back room so the other caretakers could hear Soraya ranting. The radio was silent. My mouth was hanging open. I thought: maybe Soraya will see me staring at her, and it will snap her back into reality. Didn't happen though. Soraya just kept yelling at us.

Malika ambled up around the azaleas on the edge of the parking lot and slowly kept making her way toward the front door. It seemed to take her forever. Soraya caught sight of her and started screaming even louder, careening around the reception area, bouncing off Ardelle's desk with one outstretched hand while the other braced for the wall behind her. She bounced back and forth in the hallway between the desk and the wall, yelling, yelling at Malika.

Malika finally approached the front walkway and made her way up to the door, walking almost completely upright now. For a second she looked like a human woman coming in for a job interview. She got to the front door, then stopped and sat down in front of it. She gazed at Soraya through the glass. Ardelle and I stared at her, knowing she could open the door and step inside and attack Soraya. Or either of us. She could knock us down and kick us and bite off our fingers. But she didn't. She sat there and stared, down on her haunches with her arms hanging down in front of her, a small, waiting, bonobo package.

Soraya edged up to the glass door and yelled at Malika, except now she almost started to sound sorry. After a minute she said, "I had to, Malika. I had to."

Malika just sat there and looked at her. She could have opened the door, come inside, and gotten to Soraya in two seconds. She could have, but she didn't.

17

She just groomed herself and looked out the window.

I woke up at 3:58 on a chilly Friday with their names orbiting in my head: Julian, Christine, Ardelle, with a sparkly cross around her neck and two kids in college. Kalala, gone. Demanding Imena, babylike Joie, Faraji, Uba, big and bulky. Per, who hadn't felt it important enough to come to the front of the main building and meet me officially. I lay and looked at the ceiling, and thought about how I wasn't really in my bed, in my apartment, with my husband and my child. I was in the woods, at my desk, at the lab, with Soraya, or wandering around, looking for her. I was standing at the apes' enclosure, my hands laid flat against the chain link, talking about treats. I was showing visitors around, pointing out the apes by name, waving my hands to remind the visitors to stay back, stay back.

I tried to envision walking through another day at the lab, not telling anyone what was going on. I couldn't imagine how that was supposed to work.

When I got there, I found a note in my chair from Soraya. It lay folded up in a two-inch square on my chair, thick oatmealy paper with my name in green marker ink. In the first second I saw it, waiting unguarded just past my open office door, I wondered if it was merely more notes she'd made on me that she wanted to show me. Because she'd been studying me. As if I were set of data. Or an ape.

Now I'd been carrying messages to her around in my head for so many weeks that it seemed strange that it would be so easy for her as to just jot down a note if she wanted me. I pictured her sneaking through the early morning lab light to leave it for me, and picked it up and held it like it had come from space.

Her note said she wanted to show me something, and could I stay late today. That was all.

Our apartment was really just a bed to me now, or maybe a closet somewhere to come to change clothes in the dark. It helped if I could get there after dark and stay under the covers until Marc left. He hadn't cooked for me in weeks, wouldn't look at me, and when I saw him he shot me hateful looks, baleful looks, accusing without saying a word. So I never even called him to say I'd be late. I just made plans to stay.

I spent most of the day in my office, reconciling the credit card accounts to the receipts. If a receipt was missing, I marked it with red check and didn't try to find it. On an ordinary day I'd have gone knocking on office doors, entreating people to look in their bags, search the floors of their cars, find receipts for ape toys and chow, blankets and balls, medicine, bleach to clean the cages. The lab was closing. Receipts didn't matter now.

But I needed the hours of rote paperwork to take my mind off seeing Soraya later, to wonder what she wanted me for, to imagine what she'd say. She didn't say where we were to meet or when exactly. I was terrified she'd suddenly want me again after so many weeks, or that she wouldn't, or that she'd forget the whole thing.

The thought that she might remember, that she'd show up and we'd go off together, back into the woods somewhere, kept returning as I made my notes. Electricity sparked up my still-hurt spine. I tried to put that energy back into the numbers, leaving notes for the lab's future anthropologists in the logs. I wanted to show all of them that we'd all done our best here. I wanted the red checks to show a restrained protest that even the accountants downtown might recognize someday.

For God's sake, I thought, making my little red check marks, we communicated with apes around here. We collected data on them and drove them around in SUVs. We spent our days reaching out to beings from an alternate universe, a sentient species so much more human than we are. So no, sorry, in fact we could not keep track of every receipt from WalMart.

On page 38 of the 71-page log, I took my red pen and, very neatly in the top right hand corner of the page, wrote "Fuck You."

I was sitting staring out the window when 4:00 came, and suddenly Soraya's head poked around my open office door.

"Are you ready?"

I gasped. Then I tried to make it look as though I'd been concentrating and she'd startled me, but she never even noticed, she just started right in. She came and sat down in the other chair.

The first thing I noticed was that she was sunburned. She'd kept the Earth Mover over her allotted time, spending days rooting around in the woods. She smelled like warm dirt and leaves. Pine straw hung from the bottom of her washed-out red men's waffle-weave shirt, the sleeves creeping halfway up her forearms, the kind miners wore in Tennessee or something, red strings hanging down here and there. As she sat, as her body floated down in the chair so close to me, I smelled her. I could smell her stale sweat, her unwashed hair. It was exhilarating. It felt like falling.

She had kissed me and told me she wanted me and then went and kept notes on me like I was a frog in formaldehyde. She'd been coming apart for awhile before I'd ever met her. Now she was perched in the office chair next to me, hands in her lap and her shoulders up around her ears, like a kid at Christmas. Suddenly I felt like stalling her, to give me some time to catch up and be ready for whatever she might throw at me.

"I am not going out on the front loader thing, Soraya," I shot out, a spoiled brat again, terrified in that second that she'd just get up and leave again but not able to stop myself. "What were you doing out there? You tore the hell out of the woods, did you know that?"

I hated the sound of my voice, could not believe I was haranguing her. I hadn't seen her in so long and just wanted to hold her, and suddenly I was yelling. It was like watching someone else.

She was unfazed, though. She kept smiling, rearing back a little in the chair, and just waited for me to stop.

Then: "Don't worry about the woods. We're not going on the front loader. I'm taking you in with the apes tonight."

I'd been clenching my mouth shut, and when she said that it fell and hung open.

"Me? Why?"

She shrugged.

"Because it's time. Because you're ready. The apes will accept you now."

I just looked at her, at the dirt encrusted on the wrinkles around her eyes.

"I…what does that even mean? I don't want to go in with the

apes," I mewled. The idea of stalling didn't occur to me now. I was on a moving train. She was going to bring me in with the apes. Just Soraya and me. And the apes.

I leaned forward and squinted into her eyes, waiting for the reasons I couldn't do it to surface so I could list them to her. There were many. Weren't there? I just sat looking at her. She took that as excitement, acquiescence. She didn't seem to care much how I felt about it. She just held out her hand to me.

She assumed that since going in with the apes was all Christine, Julian, Uba — anybody at the lab — ever wanted, it was what I wanted too. All I wanted at that moment was to be with her, and to me being with the apes was not even secondary, but very far down the list. I was perfectly happy dealing with them through the chain link. Going in hadn't ever occurred to me.

I wanted to ask if she was ready for them to bite me, if she'd thought about that, if it was likely. I wondered if I was bitten, could I get another job involving the use of a laptop? Would they bite the tips of my fingers like Kalala, or would they go for the whole hand?

"I don't want to go in with the apes, Soraya," I said, but then realized I hadn't said that at all, just screamed it in my head. What if they all just decided to attack me – because I was too close to Soraya, or too apart from her, anything. What if I was killed? Chloe wouldn't have a mother. But Chloe didn't have much of a mother now.

I realized that I couldn't give voice to that now. It would make us both too afraid. It would make the worst happen. I went cold and my chest went tight. But I put my hand in hers and we stood up and walked to the back of the building and the ape enclosure.

I'd never realized before just how many locked doors stood between us and the apes. We walked down the long hallway through a simple wooden door, then another, then a reinforced steel door, her many keys hanging from a silver circle, jangling against her thigh. The last door was heavy; she put her whole body into opening it, and held it open for me. She was smaller than me, and I ducked to pass under her arm, smelling her again.

I remember thinking, all I have to do is stop before I go through the door, I can pull up short and look her in the eye and say I can't do this, and then I can go back to my office and back home to my apartment. Marc wouldn't even have started dinner yet. There was time. But I didn't.

We went through a chain-link hallway and another heavy door, opened with two separate keys. Soraya opened them by rote, leaning into the locks, throwing them open with her shoulders.

When we got to the room where Imena lay on a swatch of outdoor carpeting, inspecting her nails, and Soraya heard me catch my breath and stumble over the threshold, she said softly, in my ear, "Don't worry. They won't try anything with you while I'm around. It'll be just fine."

Then she pointed to another batch of carpets stacked in a pile against the wall. Imena lay on one side of them and Faraji sat playing with Joie on the other. We walked in, and Soraya threw her arms wide and hooted greetings at them.

"Look, everybody, Deb's here! Deb's inside with us! It's her first time!" She swung around like she was dancing, giving me my entry, introducing me like a reality show contestant. "Let's all tell Deb how glad we are to see her!"

Faraji vocalized then, a huge hoot that started low and then went completely nuts, like a helicopter propeller, ending so loud and high I covered my ears. I felt myself laughing but I couldn't hear it. Joie jumped up and down, landing on the red ball, which went flying over to Imena, who looked up and regarded me coolly.

Soraya pointed at the blankets between them. "So Deb and I are gonna sit right down there, okay?" It was an ape heads-up as well as a warning. She moved slowly and made eye contact with all three apes as she moved forward. She reached back and took my hand again, and we made our way to the blankets.

When I sat down and turned around to take in the whole room, I noticed with a start that Malika was also in the room, in the far corner with one of the babies, nursing. She groomed him listlessly and looked off out the window, to the grass play area outside.

We were completely surrounded, totally of their world. We were hanging out while the apes groomed and played. I would say it was like being in my own living room, except I never did just hang out there. When I was home I was doing laundry, cutting up food for Chloe, paying bills, forever jumping up and putting shoes and jackets away, wiping things up with paper towels. Here we were supposed to sit, sit and just be.

Joie went crazy. He bounded over to me and sat on my legs. He put his hands on my shoulders and peered into my eyes, his brown rimmed in deepest black, his face a wide, bright smile. He pursed his lips at me, a thin, brown cardboard kiss that stuck a half inch in front of his face when he squeezed them together like that. I wanted to kiss him back. He seemed like he would let me. I leaned forward and did it, and the long black hairs on his face made my nose itch.

For those few minutes it felt relatively okay. It felt like visiting older relatives you don't know well, who put up with your impromptu visit because they would hate to be rude, so they put out storebought cookies and sit in the living room staring at you. You sit on the couch, your heart pounding up into your throat, your every movement an electrical prick up your spine, not daring to breathe, your eyes on the floor, scared that they secretly plan to eat you.

Soraya got up and put "Home Alone" in the VCR and we all sat quietly together for a few minutes, watching Macaulay Culkin run around. She sat there with me, about four feet away, cross-legged with her back against the wall like me. She made chitchat with Imena but didn't acknowledge Malika, who seemed to return her disdain.

This is what they all want, I thought. Christine and Julian and Uba and Clara, this is what brings them to this lab every day, what they give all their time and energy in service to. Watching "Home Alone" with apes.

And in another moment of clarity: this is not what I want. I want to watch movies at home with my child. I am supposed to be home with my child. Right now, now before I'm killed.

Soraya went into the kitchen after a few minutes and busied herself making a snack for the apes, pulling out salad greens Christine had put in the refrigerator for them, washing grapes and blueberries, doling everything out into small plastic bowls. I watched her, wondering if she'd done that for the son she never saw anymore. How old was he? Where was he? Why did she never talk about him and why did we never see him? Why had she replaced him with apes?

I watched Soraya's every move, thought how she seemed to forget the apes were even there, thinking they were involved in watching the movie. And there was something I remember only now, after everything went down and was bigger and badder than I ever thought to be afraid of, after I finally got well again, I remembered only recently that I realized Imena was watching me. Only pretending to look after Joie and watch the movie and be interested in what Faraji and Malika were doing. Watching me watch Soraya. For probably 15 minutes she watched me, warned me, and I never saw it until the last second.

What I remembered immediately was that feeling of being

at the top of the stairs, of knowing you're going to fall, and that second stretches out into hours, like you could look down and watch yourself fall in slow motion, smell the dust as you kick it up and hear your own bones breaking, all of it broadcast into your brain before you ever even started to fall.

I finally felt Imena's glare and snapped my neck around to the right to look at her, feeling the fear in my face. Realizing too late I never should have let her see me like that, looking down and then not being able to help myself, looking back up to see if she was coming for me. She was. But then from my left came a force I never saw, a black arm the size of a piano picking me up and slamming me back against the wall, and then it all went dark.

18

She's waking up.

I woke up on a stretcher in the hallway of the hospital. Marc was there, leaning against the wall, staring up at the ceiling. My head was made of pain, it was a big black curtain that I tried to nudge aside to open my eyes. I flitted my eyelashes at it in slow motion a few times, letting in some light.

Christine's voice started up to my left, and I moved my eyes a few inches to see her standing in the hallway beside me. It made my brain feel like it would spill out of my skull. I probably groaned. It's hard to remember all the details.

"Marc," Christine said softly. "She's waking up."

I don't recall Marc saying much in response. Christine moved so that I didn't have to look up to see her and leaned over me. She reached for both my hands.

I realized she and Marc hadn't ever met before now. Where was Chloe? Someone told me once they didn't let very young children visit people in the hospital.

"I'm…I'm really glad you woke up," Christine said, letting all the pent-up air out of her lungs but still whispering, chuckling a little in that girlish way she had.

I wasn't sure where we were yet or why and I felt furtive, like we'd snuck in. It felt as though, if you were in a car accident or had a heart attack or something else normal you were taken in an ambulance to the hospital, treated like a person, given an actual room, but if you snuck inside an ape enclosure against every university insurance and safety regulation in the eight-inch thick binder on the shelf in my office, they most likely whisked you into the back of a dirty unmarked animal van, hoping nobody called 911, and carried you into the ER through a back door where you hung out in the hall with no actual hospital personnel anywhere.

I think I asked where Chloe was. I hope I did.

"You've been out for over an hour," Christine said.

Marc came and stood behind her then. There was something I wanted to ask them but I couldn't think of what it was.

That's one thing I remember from that night, that everyone else did the talking. For the moment I focused on Christine's face and she was saying that they didn't think I was hurt too badly, but they were waiting to get me fully checked out in the ER. The lights were too bright in the hallway, and my ears were ringing.

She told me what Soraya had reported to her: that Imena had started coming for me and meant to bite me. She meant to attack me. Christine told me this part quickly but that's the part that has stuck the longest. That's just how she put it: Imena was coming for me. Imena was going to kill me.

But she didn't make it. Faraji had seen what was happening, and he was only about six feet from me on the other side, sitting with his back to the wall like I was. So while I stared at Imena, shocked, immobile, Faraji scooted over and pushed me out of the way. Soraya had told Christine it looked like he was going to try push me forward, and then run behind me along the wall, to get between Imena and me. But I didn't see him and so I didn't move in the right way, and in the scuffle I fell backward instead, and he knocked my head against the wall.

"Soraya called me on the radio, and Julian and I came and found you and you were out cold," she said, taking another long breath. "But there was no blood or anything….Oh my God —"

Just then she realized I didn't remember any of it. This was the first I was hearing of Imena wanting to attack me. I didn't remember getting shoved against the wall. I was passed out and they put me in the van and brought me to the hospital. I didn't know what had happened. Christine thought I was afraid I'd been bitten, but I didn't even think to look down at my hands. If Imena had bitten me, she would have had to go for my head, because that's what hurt.

"It's okay. She didn't bite you. She didn't get near you. Faraji didn't let her. Faraji saved you. You just hit your head. She didn't bite you, Deb. You have a head injury. That's all."

Christine let out all her breath again, trying to feel in control of things. She teared up a little then and looked off down the hall.

Marc looked at Christine like she was an alien, and she bristled and leaned away. He leaned in past her, over my stomach, and pointedly made eye contact with me then, asked me if I felt okay. I must have nodded, because I thought he started to look relieved.

A little while later, somebody in green scrubs came up, a thin, late twentysomething man with red hair and freckles like a grown-up Opie, and Christine and Marc moved back to let him through. He put one hand over mine, leaned over the stretcher and peered into my face like they had, holding my eyelids open with his thumbs, clicking a penlight and shining it in my eyes, the light like a knife.

"Hi," he said. "You're awake, that's good."

He checked my pulse on his watch as he talked. Then he

patted my hands with his, a light, dry touch of white, freckled fingers.

"You've had what we call a mild traumatic brain injury. We used to call them concussions. It's a closed injury, which means the skull is not involved. No fracture that we can see. No gross structural changes to the brain. You've got just a little laceration in the back there, nothing that's going to give you too much trouble. There's some swelling, which we would expect from the type of blunt injury you've got. I don't really see any brain damage or anything like that."

Brain damage? I blinked at him. But he was saying there was no brain damage. Oh. Okay.

"Anyway, we're going to get you an MRI and keep you here overnight just to make sure you don't have any other problems, but you should be able to go home tomorrow. Maybe Sunday. Can you tell me what day it is today?"

That was hard. I believe I told him it was getting cold outside. He frowned.

"Ok, well, I'll ask you again in a bit. Do you have a headache?"

I think I closed my eyes in response. He told me to just relax and they'd get me into a room soon. They told me later I tried to sit up then, that I groaned a lot and asked where Chloe was. I remember looking down at the floor, expecting to see her toddling up to see me. She had curly blonde hair like mine that she never let anyone brush, and always carried a stuffed dolphin around everywhere. Funny I hadn't thought about that dolphin in forever. I carried an image of my baby girl around in my head every minute, so it didn't hurt so much that I never actually spent any time with her. But I'd forgotten about the dolphin. I never saw the dolphin anymore. It was raggedy and dirty with the stitches starting to come out, and thinking about it now made me see that I hadn't been with my girl in days, weeks. "Anybody sees a little blonde girl in a corduroy jumper from Target with a stuffed dolphin, send her in here," I wanted to say, but I can't remember if I said it out loud or not.

...

I woke up later in a room, a beige canvas sheet separating me from my hospital roommate, Marc beside my bed, watching Jeopardy in a plastic chair.

"Where's Chloe?" I asked him.

His head swiveled on his neck and he looked at me. He squinted like he was trying to see if I was really awake. Then he reached for the remote and switched off the TV. He came over to sit in the plastic chair next to my hospital bed.

"You've been asking that a lot tonight," he said, his lips and teeth tight, his hair needing a wash, his cell-phone selling polo still on from work.

"She's with a babysitter," he said evenly. "Like she has been for about 80 percent of the time you've had this fucking job. How's your head?"

"It hurts," I whined, a baby myself.

Marc leaned forward in his chair, a hand on each knee. He looked at his knees instead of at me. I watched him stare at his knees.

I thought he must know everything now. Christine had told him I'd gone in with the apes. He'd probably figured out himself that I'd been falling in love with someone at the lab, and after Christine's story, he'd figured it was Soraya. I wondered how much he knew, if he was disturbed that I'd fallen in love with a woman, if he even knew Soraya's name.

Slowly, rhythmically, he rubbed his hands on his knees. He stared at my feet in the bed. He wouldn't look at my face.

"Are you ready?" He asked me.

I remember trying to figure out what he was talking about. I think I just squinted at him again.

"I said, are you ready?" Now he was standing at my bedside peering down at me.

"Ready for what?" I croaked.

"For what I'm going to tell you," he said quietly.

"What are you going to tell me?" I thought: You know everything. I have a concussion. I don't have enough problems?

"I'm going to tell you what's going to happen now. And you're going to listen. Are you ready?"

So this was how it was all ending. I'd crashed the car. He was driving now.

"First, you're going to get out of here tomorrow, and you're going to come home. Then, if you go back to that lab on Monday, I'm going to take Chloe and leave you. The same day. The same hour. Do you understand?"

I was crying suddenly, and I couldn't see him. My head hurt so much I didn't think to move my hands to wipe the tears. They just filled my eyes up until I felt like I was drowning.

"I don't know what is going on with you and that woman, and I don't care," he said, still so slowly, evenly, quietly. "I'm telling you once more. You go back, we leave. You got it?"

It hurt more with every word. I said okay, one small word, feeble as a kitten. Marc looked at the thin blue hospital blanket on my bed, at his plastic chair. He wouldn't look at me.

He didn't realize the lab was closing. I told him.

"Well, what is that supposed to mean to me, Deb?" he asked, still looking at the blanket. "I don't know anything about that place. You haven't told me anything about what you do all day since this summer. I figured it all out on my own. We haven't had a conversation of any kind, beyond taking care of Chloe, for the last three months."

He needed a few minutes to think, and I took them to will away the pain in my head. He sat back down on the chair and I closed my eyes. Then through the black behind my eyelids he said:

"Does the woman here — Christine — know the lab's closing? Where will the apes go?"

I kept crying. I could feel the back of my head where I hit the wall, all my pain coming from there, from Faraji, from Soraya, from Imena. From their parting blows, shoving me out when I thought I was getting in.

Now Marc was crying too, in his plastic chair.

"It's just too dangerous, Deb," he whispered. "It's almost like you want to get killed. Do you want to get killed? For that woman? For a job?"

Then he got up and paced my hospital room.

"That woman —" he pointed out the open door to the hallway, where we'd last seen Christine. "She was missing the top part of two of her fingers. Did an ape do that?"

He waited for an answer. I didn't say anything.

"And so somebody decides to open up the cage door for you and you *go in there*?" he spat at me. "Why? For this Soraya person? Seriously?"

I was able to move my head, very slowly, enough to look out the window.

He kept going. He went back and sat down in his chair, and started repeating himself, ever so quietly.

"You will not go back there," he whispered, shaking a little. "Not ever. Not even to get your stuff."

I stared out the window.

"You've never told me what to do before," I said flatly.

"You've never endangered your life before, idiot," he spat.

"You've never cheated on me before. I knew who you were before."

Who was that? I thought.

Then the conversation was over and yet another decision had been taken out of my hands, made while I was still wondering what was going on.

I had an MRI. I was fine. They didn't have to strap me down.

Soraya didn't visit me in the hospital.

Marc had called my mother, and she was on her way from New York. She was there by the next morning, sleeping on the couch when we walked in from the hospital at 9 a.m.

Chloe was still lying on her back, asleep in her crib. I stopped in front of her room and leaned against the doorway. My movement woke her, and she opened her beautiful ocean eyes and smiled at me, humming a little tune. We just looked at each other for a minute.

I thought maybe she was welcoming me back.

Marc brushed past me in the hallway. He stopped and gently pulled me out of her room.

"She does that every day," he said. "She wakes up, singing like that, every day. With no help from you. She's her own little person. You're not going to break her."

I went back in and stared dully at Chloe, drowning again. How ridiculous of me to think he didn't know, that I'd kept how afraid I was of Chloe a secret. Marc shared a bed with me. He could see me. And he held up a mirror so I could see myself, a white square cotton bandage held with sticky tape to the back of my head and blood still in my hair.

…

Christine called me Sunday night. She'd called Dr. Dorn's office to report my injury Friday night while I was still unconscious. He'd told her about the lab's closing.

"Soraya called me Saturday morning. They'd told her and she was freaking out. Screaming about them taking the apes away."

"You told me it would happen that way," I said, my voice a monotone.

"Yes," Christine said. "Listen, that's not all. She called me that night after midnight. She was freaked that they're planning to take the apes away. She took a bunch of pills, Deb. An overdose. She tried to kill herself."

I couldn't breathe. I was going to throw up.

"So Julian and I went to her house in the middle of the night, and we put her in the Tahoe. We took her to the hospital to have her stomach pumped. She's there now. If you want to visit, or something."

Christine heard me gasping. I couldn't speak.

"She's done it before," she hurried to tell me. "Last year. She broke up with some guy. Her son did something to piss her off. Who knows."

I didn't say anything for a second. I tried to get control of my breathing.

"It wasn't…" I started.

Me?

No. It wasn't me.

We had to let the truck go first.

They came to take the apes away on a freezing Tuesday in January at 6:30 in the morning. It was spitting rain and barely light out. By the time I got to the lab, Soraya had already handcuffed herself to the gate.

I got out of my car and went straight to her. I felt slow, sleepy, shocked awake. I hadn't seen Soraya in months. She'd cut off all her hair – hacked it off, from the looks of it. It looked like spiky brownies. Little beads of rain settled on the pieces of hair that stood straight up, and sleep was still in her eyes.

She knelt by the gate with her arms stretched out above her head. She looked dirty, like she'd been up all night. She didn't have shoes on. One black flip-flop laid upside-down near her, but I didn't know if it was hers.

Two girls, her students, were also handcuffed to the chain-link fence on either side of her in sweaters and yellow plastic ponchos, in solidarity. But they were much younger than us and they looked better kept up. They greeted me politely when I walked up, called me ma'am.

There were some other people hanging around next to the gate, maybe a dozen in groups of two and three, friends of Soraya's that I'd shown around the lab once or twice before. They drank from paper cups of coffee and watched to see what she would do.

I went to her and opened my mouth to speak, but she spoke first. I looked back over my shoulder to see a reporter packed into a light-blue suit getting out of a TV news van.

"The truck's not here yet, but it'll be here soon. You want to get the whole thing on tape. Please," she called past me. "Help me stop them."

She sounded crazy. I stopped in my tracks then and saw: she also looked a little crazy. She wore jeans and a dark grey hooded sweatshirt with the lab's white logo and an imprint of apes scampering across the back. The lab assistants all had them too, but theirs were well worn from having been on their backs while they cleaned the ape enclosures with bleach solution. Soraya's was new, like she'd maybe grabbed it on her way out the door that morning from the office supply closet, where I used to store the new ones until people bought them. In fact, the more I looked the more I knew that's exactly what she'd done. She looked at me now like she knew what I was thinking, like she was unrepentant.

I came up a little closer, searching her face for signs that she knew me, that she loved me. There were none. So I stopped where I was, about ten feet away from her, staring and sick.

Things were finally starting to fall apart for Soraya. Everything her critics had forewarned was coming true. A crazy growing forcefield surrounded her now, its thick, grey air pushing us apart. Soraya blinked the rainy mist out of her violet eyes and glared up at the sky.

I could see now that decline was well underway by the time I came to the lab to work for her, months before, when it was still hot out and we would walk the trails of the lab grounds in shorts, pulling up wild onions for the apes to eat. The woman I met then had a reputation on campus as brilliant but difficult, wrote beautiful papers on apes' communicative and cultural abilities but was starting to have trouble making herself understood by her own human assistants.

There was still someone in there, someone I had loved. But I couldn't see her anymore.

The graduate students told horror stories about Soraya but still clamored to get close to her as they could. Her eyes had been clear and open as a child's, she could see things other people couldn't. But by the time I left, just before Christmas, I felt like I couldn't get through to her at all, and she never seemed to understand what I was telling her. It was like constantly living in that silent, expansive second before a car crash.

Now it was winter. Now we were all staring at a barefoot lunatic handcuffed to a chain-link fence, watching, helpless as she opened her mouth to yell.

"Dr. Baldwin, can we ask you some questions?" the girl reporter said, her blue suit and coiffed hair an insult to the raw surroundings. She moved like she was chasing Soraya through a crowd, like she was working hard to get an interview with a famous scientist who didn't have much time and might get away quickly, though Soraya had called herself to tell the TV station about what was to happen that morning, and she wasn't going anywhere. Knowing her, she probably didn't have the key to the handcuffs.

The reporter reached Soraya and knelt down in front of her in heels and pencil skirt. I didn't hear what she asked. But Soraya's voice sang out, and given how she looked I thought she sounded relatively sane.

"These apes are my family. They're my intellectual property. I've worked with them here in this lab for more than 20 years. I cannot allow them to be shipped away. I will not allow it."

Soraya glared at the reporter then, as if it were she who wanted to take the apes away. The reporter, still kneeling, swiveled around a bit to look into the face of the camera, held by an also kneeling cameraman. The three of them looked like they were praying together. I crept a little closer until I could hear her clearly:

"Soraya Ruhl, a psychologist who has cared for the apes at this Southern University primate facility for more than 20 years, chained herself to a gate this morning at the research center, which is located on 50 acres of university-owned land south of Atlanta.

"Ruhl has been recognized worldwide for her research, which has demonstrated that bonobo apes have the ability to communicate with human beings and each other. She's taught them rudimentary reading and showed that the animals exhibited both caring and culture.

"As you can see," the girl reporter stood up then and the cameraman stood with her. She swept her blue-clad arm up over her head to alert the audience to the whole gate, "about a dozen activists have joined Dr. Ruhl, some also chaining themselves to the gate."

She looked back over her shoulder at the buildings just on the other side of the gate.

"A week ago, university officials announced they would close down this lab because Dr. Ruhl has been unable to find additional funds to support her research. Yesterday, she asked Federal District Judge Leonard Brooks for a temporary restraining order to halt the apes' transfer."

She paused here, looked right at me for just a second. I was the only one standing close to Soraya and I wondered if she'd want to know why. I was trying to keep my face blank, afraid she'd come over and start asking me questions next, afraid she'd catch my fear and hate of the whole situation bubbling up and want to watch it boil over. But she was really just looking off camera for a moment for drama's sake.

"Just last night, word came that Dr. Ruhl's request was denied."

She's actually pretty swift for a local TV news reporter, I thought. Then she did look over and seemed to pointedly see me. She handed her mic off to some guy standing nearby and moved toward me. Then she was in front of me, blocking my view of Soraya. I'm farsighted, and she stood too close. I blinked and squinted, shook my head to clear it.

"Do you know Dr. Baldwin? Dr. Ruhl? Actually," she leaned in then so I couldn't make out her face at all, lowered her voice to an apologetic whisper, "I'm sorry – but which name does she go by?"

"She goes by both names. Soraya Baldwin-Ruhl. Hyphenated," I answered slowly and carefully, a huge hand squeezing my insides as I said her name.

"Do you work with her?" the reporter asked, too brightly.

"I used to," I said. I was peering around the reporter to catch sight of Soraya again. She moved to block my view. I caught myself and stuck out my hand.

"I'm sorry," I said. "I'm Deborah Solomon. I worked as the lab's business manager until a few months ago." At the moment I looked nothing like a business manager of anything, in sweats and sneakers and a jean jacket, long, curly, unruly dirty-blonde bedhead, no makeup or coffee.

"I'm sorry again," I said, pointing at my clothes. "It's early for me."

"It's nice to meet you, Deb," she said, shaking my hand. Our hands were stiff and cold. "Do you mind if I ask why you left?"

I should've probably expected the question, but I had no answer for her. I'd gotten a call last night that they were coming for the apes today, that there would probably be press and that Soraya would probably be acting crazy, that she'd threatened to off herself right there as they loaded the apes onto the truck. I'd quit right after my accident, but when they called me, I came.

Then we heard the truck coming up the road and turned to watch it rumble up and stop in front of the gate.

When you anticipate these things, you can't help thinking that the scene's going to be shouting, shoving, things getting out of hand quickly, like in a movie. But it was all very quiet. A man got out of the truck and walked up to Soraya. She looked right in his face and said, "I won't let you take them."

He grinned down at her.

"That's fine, ma'am," he said, actually holding his hands up and taking two steps back. "I can wait a few minutes."

He was big with a blonde crewcut and wore a camo t-shirt — which made me think suddenly that the scene did in fact look a lot we were in a movie, or at least he was.

That's when the cops showed up, something like five or six cruisers sent by the Sheriff's office. They drove in slowly, quietly, parked there in front of the gate and walked up to the camo guy. They all carried themselves as though they didn't want trouble, wanted to be nice, didn't stare at everybody chained to the gate.

All the arrivals took a few minutes, and the reporter and Soraya and the protestors spoke quietly to each other, but I couldn't hear what anybody was saying. I couldn't tell what Soraya was thinking but I don't think she had expected any cops.

The men walked past the reporter and cameraman like they didn't see them, and approached Soraya. They started talking to her then, finishing up the conversation they'd already started.

"The thing is, Dr. Ruhl, if you persist in blocking our entrance to the facility, we'll need to arrest you. We don't have any choice," one of them said.

There were so many of them by then, short and tall, skinny and wide, all dressed in tan uniforms, some with very official-looking Sheriff's hats like Smokey the Bear. They towered over Soraya, who was still kneeling, still chained to the gate.

"Now, here is what needs to happen, Ms. Ruhl," said a Sheriff's deputy who seemed to function as foreman. "This gentleman here needs to drive his truck through the gate. Then he and his associates are going to load the apes onto the truck and drive them to a facility in Texas, where they're going to be cared for. While they do this, my fellow deputies and I will stay here and make sure everything goes nice and smooth, okay?"

Soraya looked down at the sandy ground and shook her head slowly.

"Ms. Ruhl, I do need to remind you that this has all been arranged."

He looked down at her. We all watched her, motionless, and she just looked up at him.

"Now, for all this to happen, you need to release yourself from this gate, and you need to let all your friends here know you want them to do the same."

"You need to let us do our job," the camo guy said.

Another graduate student of Soraya's, Emily, walked up to her then. She was dressed like a wacky New Ager, a waifish woman dressed like Stevie Nicks with flowing skirts under a lab t-shirt, Teva sandals and long, wavy reddish hair. She'd threatened to leave back in the fall; I didn't know why she was still around. She knelt at the gate and put a hand over the one Soraya had sticking into the chain-link.

"Soraya, I think it might be better if you were with these guys when they took the apes. Let Faraji and Imena know it's okay.

Make sure nobody gets hurt getting onto the truck," she said.

Soraya just looked at her feet.

I felt myself walking up to her then. I hadn't planned it, but then I was at the gate and staring at Soraya's hands in the handcuffs. She'd already unlocked them, if they were ever really locked, and she dropped her hands to her lap.

I knelt about six feet from her in the grass next to the fence. I could touch her if I wanted. If she would let me.

"Soraya, I think…this is over," I said, looking back over my shoulder at the building where the apes were waiting to start their day. I'm sure they didn't realize they'd be leaving for Texas today, but the days leading up to this one had probably been very tense, and I was sure they'd picked up on it. I looked back at my own car, where my husband and child waited for me. I'd wanted to come alone today to help out, and that had been disallowed.

"It's not over. It can't be over," she told me. "These apes are my property. These guys think they can come take them in some….some commando raid?"

I thought, it's funny: she doesn't really look like she's out of her mind. She looked intense, like she was in the middle of a big project. Focused, ears perked up like an animal's with attention to detail. Soft eyes, intelligent, set back over high cheekbones. She smiled at me like she didn't know who I was. I just looked back at her, until I couldn't anymore.

"Soraya. They're taking the apes today, and if you try to stop them, they're going to arrest you," I said.

She didn't look at me or Emily. She just let all the air out of her chest in one loud gust and then stood up, slowly and methodically, like a very old person. Then she just let the handcuffs slip off her lap onto the ground, and walked to the gate to open it.

Again I kept thinking about what this scene would look like in the movie version: maybe some of her friends would also release their own handcuffs and walk over to her, put an arm around her, hug her. Maybe the actress playing Soraya would make a speech of some kind, or cry silently as the music swelled, her eyes shining as the tears streamed down her dirt-streaked face. None of that happened. Nobody approached her as she punched her security code into the metal box and stood back to wait for the gate to swing open.

She walked through it alone, still barefoot, making her way to the ape building, looking down at the ground. Then we all walked in behind her, but we had to let the truck go first.

Acknowledgements, etc.

Thank you Steve MacQueen, Pam Ball, Diane Roberts, Jan Pudlow, Charles Badland, David Morris, Kim Round, Bethany Round, Richard Brunck, Kati Schardl, Don Quarello and Beverly Frick, for absolutely everything.

This book is dedicated to Steve, Claire and Rose MacQueen.

www.ingramcontent.com/pod-product-compliance
Lightning Source LLC
Chambersburg PA
CBHW070118260626
47160CB00004B/1516